This special signed
edition is limited to
1000 numbered copies.

This is copy 530 .

JOE R. LANSDALE

JOHN L. LANSDALE

HELL'S BOUNTY

HELL'S BOUNTY

JOE R. LANSDALE

JOHN L. LANSDALE

SUBTERRANEAN PRESS 2016

First Edition

ISBN
978-1-59606-745-5

Subterranean Press
PO Box 190106
Burton, MI 48519

subterraneanpress.com

In memory of a real horror fan.
Patsy Pugh, this one is for you.
J.L.L.

To everyone who ever enjoyed a good,
old-fashioned pulp-style story with wooly
boogers and cowboys, blood and dust,
ropes and bullets, fire and carnage,
and a whisper of Armageddon.
J.R.L.

So Satan called up his minions, counted them one by one. And the worst of them was missing.
FROM *THE BOOK OF DOCHES*

PART ONE:

A Whiff of Sulfur

By the pricking of my thumbs, something wicked this way comes.
SHAKESPEARE'S *MACBETH*

A full moon hung at the peak of a shadowy mountain like a gold coin on a pedestal, shining thin light into the narrow canyon below. Above it all, shimmering white dots filled the dark velvet sky. A lone wolf's howl echoed across the canyon as if it were trying to call up the dead. When the howl faded, the ground began to shake, rumbling louder and louder.

At the summit of a narrow, rising grade, an old boarded up mine shaft trembled and dripped dirt. The boards in front of the mine cracked and blew out in a spin of splinters and dust. A dark cloud coughed out of the shaft, soared toward the sky, temporarily blotted out the moon. The cloud tore apart with a screech, burst into a horde of chattering bats flying in all directions, once again revealing the gold doubloon moon.

The bats flew a short distance, merged, and raced toward a smattering of lights from the town of Falling Rock. In one elegant swoop they dove, soared above the dusty street that centered the town, fluttered past the sound of a plinking piano and shrill laughter spilling out of the dimly lit Sundown Saloon.

Horses out front, tied to the hitching post, began to snort. The twisted mass of bats rose up and appeared to swim through the sky, toward a church belfry, toward the tall bell tower there, gathered in it thick as wet rot, and once collected there, there was a puffing sound and a thick twirl of black shadow. The shadow hardened, formed a dark image with eyes like wounds. Wings flapped from the shape's back, gathered up moonlight and folded it into the wings and tossed it out again. It flexed its hands and took in a breath so deep the night sky seemed to shudder.

With a flip of a dark hand, a small box became visible. With a touch of its other hand, the box lid sprang open and red lights jumped out of the box like inflamed grasshoppers. The lights twisted into odd shapes and the little shapes darted about the tower and ricocheted off the huge bell like gunfire. Then they slowed and went for the inside of the bell and clung to it, hissed like ants on a hot skillet, burned themselves into its interior. Finally, they were still and the hissing stopped and the glowing stopped and what they left imprinted deep in the metal of the bell were hieroglyphic-like impressions.

The shadowy thing snapped the box closed and let out with a sound like it had just eaten something tasty. The box was deftly put away and the great winged shadow leaped from the tower, fell for a long distance, then flapping its leathery wings, rose up against the moonlight briefly, sailed away, filling the air with a whiff of sulfur.

The bat wings of the Sundown Saloon cracked open and a little man flew through them, out into the street, another man's boot flashing at the end of his ass. The little man's bowler hat came loose from his head and rolled around in the dirt before lying down with a wobble.

The man who had kicked the little man came into the street. He had a smashed hat in one hand and a bottle in the other. He looked mean enough to eat floor tacks and shit horseshoes.

"You little worm," the mean man said. "Ain't nobody sits on Trumbo Quill's hat."

The man in the street hiked a leg under him and made it to his feet. He eyed his hat but decided against it. He took off running.

Taking his time, Trumbo Quill put his hat on his head and pulled his revolver and fired. The little man, who had actually covered a pretty good patch of ground, threw his leg forward in what looked like a goose step, did a stumble step, and went to one knee. He hung there for a moment then fell on his face in the dusty street and rolled on his back. He set up and took hold of his knee. The bullet had gone through the back of his leg and popped loose the knee cap, splintered it. There was a hole there big enough to hide a plum.

Quill came and stood over the little man and said, "How're you feelin'?"

"God, Quill. You done ruined my knee."

"I'd say the whole leg, wouldn't you? Your dancin' days is over, if you ever had any."

"I can't walk. You've ruined me."

"I think you're right. Well, can't leave you that way."

Quill lifted the pistol and fired. The shot took off the top of the little man's head.

"See," Quill said. "All better now."

Quill lifted the bottle in his other hand and finished it off. Without moving toward the saloon, he yelled out, "Hey, Double Shot, bring me another bottle."

After a moment the bat wings moved and a tall, skinny, near bald man moved through them, briskly made his way over to Quill. He looked down at the little dead man as he handed Quill the bottle.

Quill said, "Put it on my tab." Then he looked at the little man on the ground, back at Double Shot. "Ain't none of your kin, is he?"

Double Shot shook his head.

"That's good, cause in case you hadn't noticed, little son-of-a-bitch is dead. I'm gonna take me a walk. Have him out of the street before I get back. Nothin' I hate worse than a dead man in the street."

"Yes, sir," Double Shot said.

Double Shot went back in the saloon. Quill uncorked the new bottle with his teeth and took a jolt, went trudging back toward the saloon where the little man's bowler hat lay, and stepped on it, smashing it flat. He then turned and went up the street, pausing now and again to take a swig. At the end of the street, Quill passed a marker that said BOOT HILL.

He'd put a lot of men there and one woman. He hadn't liked her singing, caterwauling was more like it. She had sounded like a cat with a stick up its ass. Even the horny miners and cowboys in the saloon applauded when she hit the floor. She was not only a terrible singer, she'd had a face that could drop a raccoon out of a tree at twenty paces. Her piano player caught some of the blame too. He had been pretty swift, however, and he had made it to the door before Quill fired, punching a hole through the back of his head with a well placed shot. They were finding that piano man's teeth in the street for three, four days. Little boys gathered them up and put them on strings and wore them around their necks as mementos of the gun fight. There was even a little song they made up that went something like "He played the ivory teeth, but lost his in the street."

Quill thought it was a glorious shoot out. Course, only Quill had a gun. He felt it worked better that way, less tension on his behalf.

Quill went up the hill, and at its peak he came to a tombstone under a big oak that leaked shadow on the ground. Quill stopped there and took off his hat and placed it on the tombstone. He dropped to his knees and used the bottle of whisky to support himself.

To his left, unnoticed by Quill, a shadow perched on top of a nearby tombstone. It flicked its wings and twisted its head like a curious dog. It watched Quill carefully with its glowing eyes, watched as he pulled grass from around the grave, tossed it behind him.

A voice like thunder inside a cave said: "Would you like to have her back?"

Quill dropped the bottle, came to a crouch, pistol drawn, aiming between the glowing eyes. When Quill saw the thing he inhaled sharply.

"What in the hell are you?"

"You loved your wife, didn't you," said the winged shadow, the wings moving gently.

"How do you know about— What are you?"

"I'm your wish come true."

Quill cocked back the hammer of his revolver. "What wish?"

"I can give her back to you."

Quill swallowed. "No you can't."

"Oh, I can."

"I'll shoot you off there like the buzzard you are. You tauntin' son-of-a-bitch."

The shadow lifted its wings and the night air moved with the motion.

"You're just some drunk dream," Quill said.

"I can give her back."

Quill made with a sound that might have been a laugh. "If you could, I'd sell my soul."

The dark head of the shadow broke open and showed a smile. Lots of sharp teeth, yellow in the moonlight. The shadow stretched its right hand; it appeared to leak ink, and the next thing Quill knew the hand was long and then longer and it grabbed his own; the shadows from the arm dropped along the ground and flowed, and then the thing was no longer on the stone; it was standing right in front of him, holding his hand, the one gripping the pistol. He tried to pull the trigger, but the gun was taken from him as easily as a rattle from a baby and dropped to the ground.

Weak with nausea, Quill dropped to one knee and the shadow moved swiftly, drawing its claw-like hand across Quill's palm, cutting deep. Quill looked up at the shadow as it spread its wings wide, said, "Done."

"You are real," Quill said.

"Very."

"You're him…the one down there."

The thing split its face apart and showed the yellow teeth again.

"Worse."

"You took my soul?"

"Not yet. But soon. Pick up your gun."

Quill's hand shook as he picked up the revolver and stuck it in the holster. The shadow shape said, "First, your reward."

The shape turned its head and looked toward the grave Quill had been brooding over. The grave trembled and the dried dirt became soft and began to shift. There was a sound below the dirt like rats chewing wood, and then some of the dirt fell inward. There was a cracking and creaking sound and a hand shot up through the soil and the moon glistened off the tips of the broken fingernails.

Quill jumped to his feet, stumbled and fell on top of the grave. He grasped the wriggling hand. "Darlin' Jenny," he said, and then he let go and began to dig with his hands like a dog for a bone. Finally, he saw a sandy shape through a cracked slat of coffin. He grabbed at the slat, and pulled. The board groaned and broke. He tossed it aside, grabbed another piece and ripped. The body in the coffin worked from the inside, pushing, clawing, and then the shape sat up. Her dark hair dripped sand. Her eyes blinked, shedding dirt from the lids; the eyes were bright and green. The white burial gown she had worn was rotten and ripped. Her flesh went from sheet white to a healthy pink. She looked at Quill and smiled and spread her arms. When she did, most of the rotting gown fell off.

Quill lifted her near-nude body from the coffin as easily and as gently as a kitten. He started down the hill, carrying her. As he went down, she whispered something in his ear. It was hoarse, but he understood it: "I love you."

"And I love you," he said. "Without you…I…"

She pressed her hand to his lips.

And then her foot fell off.

Quill stopped. He looked at it on the ground, and then looked at her. She had an expression like a worm had just crawled up her ass, and considering where she had been, maybe it had.

And then her leg fell off.

Followed by an arm.

"Dang it," she said.

"No," Quill said.

"Sorry," she said.

Jenny's head rocked to one side, made a noise like a dog biting into a chicken bone, then her head rocked in the other direction—

—and fell off.

The rest of the body crumbled in his arms. He dropped to his knees as dirt and desiccated bone and hanks of flesh and hair fell to the ground. The wind picked up the fragments and moved them about and carried some of it away.

Quill yelled to the darkness. "You cheated me, you son-of-a-bitch. You cheated me. You lying bastard!"

Drawing his gun, Quill charged back up the hill, firing at shadows amidst the tombstones. But they weren't the shadows he wanted. He kicked at a stone, shoved over another, then fell into his wife's grave and rose up on his knees. He picked up a piece of her gown, clenched it in his fist, let out with a hoarse bellow that could be heard all the way down to the Sundown Saloon.

No one came to investigate.

(3)

The mid-day sun was dripping heat across the territory like hot honey poured from a pot. Down below, sunlight flashed on the bone-handled .44s strapped on the hips of a solitary rider and bounced off the silver conchos decorating his cowhide vest. His dead-black coat was rolled and bound on the back of his saddle.

He sat comfortably in the saddle, a long, lean whip of a man, his hat pulled down low to block out the yellow bitch of a sun. His face looked like a recently healed saddle sore with a mustache. He turned his head slightly as he rode past a sign that read: Falling Rock. One mile.

A mile later he rode into town passing the mining assay, the livery, a few other buildings, stopped in front of the saloon, swung off his horse, wrapped the reins around the hitching post, where another horse was tied, paused long enough to open up a saddle bag full of dynamite. He plucked out a stick and poked it into his belt. He stepped on the board-walk and stomped dirt off his boots, dusted his clothes with his hands. He unfastened his black coat from the back of his saddle and put it on. It made him look like an angry preacher. He adjusted his hat and went through the swinging doors and into the Sundown Saloon.

It wasn't much of a saloon. Clapboard, bullet-pocked walls, rough board floors with cracks wide enough to piss through, and from the smell of things, plenty had. There was an overturned spittoon and its contents oozed across the floor and ran between the cracks. A fly specked mirror hung on the wall behind the bar and there was one fly on duty. A wagon wheel hanging from the ceiling with half a dozen lighted oil lamps attached was the most promi-nent decoration. Still, with all those lamps lit and it being mid-day, it wasn't all that bright inside and the smell was ripe. It was like being inside a poorly ventilated dead dog. There was a doorway at the back and a curtain of beads hung over it and stairs could be glimpsed through the beads.

Patrons gave him a short look, went back to what they were doing. They were a sparse crew. The bartender was working the bar, wiping down glasses with an almost clean rag. Three men were standing at the bar. One was a kid that didn't look old enough to shave. He was decked out in fancy black clothes with a long black deacon's coat and a fancy black holster that held fancy pearl handled revolvers. The guns were so well oiled the air was filled with their smell and at that range it almost blocked out the stink of piss and the spittoon, stale farts and thrown-up whisky.

Across the way, two men wearing buckskin coats sat at a table, their out of date buffalo guns propped against the wall. A plump saloon girl sat in the lap of one of the men, playing with his long greasy hair. They were smiling at one another. Between them, they almost had a full set of teeth.

At another table a gray-haired man was face down, his hand gathered around an empty whisky bottle. A little black bag was on the floor beside his chair. At the table near his, three men were playing cards.

The new saloon entry made his way to the bar, said, "Whisky, and put it in a clean glass."

"Flies been in most of them," the bartender said.

"You should try turning them face down."

"Then you got the ants."

"Just give me a whisky, bartender."

"You can call me Double Shot. Everyone else does."

The bartender poured him one, and the man threw it back and winced. "Dog piss."

Double Shot smiled, waggled his hand as he said, "About fifty percent whisky, about fifty percent piss. Gives it bite."

"I'll say. Do me another."

The bartender poured, and the man at the bar turned and looked at the card players. One of them was a big guy. He wore a wrinkled hat that shadowed a face of cold determination. It was the kind of face that would make babies cry. The hands that held the cards had enough dirt under them to grow corn.

The bartender leaned over, said, "Big guy. That's Trumbo Quill. He had a bad night last night. Had to shoot someone, got his hat crushed, then got drunk enough to shoot up the graveyard. Word is too that he lost his favorite pocket knife. Another word, and this one to the wise. Watch him."

"That's two words."

Double Shot grinned.

"Thanks," said the man at the bar.

"We got girls upstairs. They'll do you this and do you that, you got some money."

"No thanks."

"Is that a stick of dynamite in your belt?"

"Naw. Just looks like it."

The man at the bar studied the other men at the poker table. One was thin and dressed all in black, had on a stove pipe hat. The man said to the bartender, "Don't tell me, the black suited man is the town preacher."

"Undertaker," said Double Shot.

"That fits."

"The other is some kind of Indian. Or half-breed. Shit, he might be a Mexican. None of them sort last around here long enough for us to learn their names."

The man leaned his back into the bar and studied the Indian. He had a crooked nose and a scar on his cheek that didn't look as if it got there from shaving. He wore a brown derby that was a size too small. It was pushed back on his head at a jaunty angle. A shotgun, the barrel almost completely sawed off, rested in a makeshift holster against his leg. The man at the bar smiled slightly, and then glanced at the sleeping man at the other table. The bartender saw him do that, said, "And that ain't nobody."

"Nobody?"

"Not anymore."

The man nodded slightly, finished his second drink, left some coins on the counter, and had the bartender pour a third. As the bartender was filling his glass, the kid came over. He looked at the man's revolvers, said, "Nice guns."

"My mother gave them to me."

The kid considered this, smirked. "Kind of an odd gift from a mother, don't you think?"

"You don't know my mother."

Double Shot said, "Kid, sit down, take a load off, let me bring you a drink."

"You shut up, bar keep," the kid said.

"Have it your way," Double Shot said, and grabbed a rag and went down the length of the bar wiping.

"Is that a stick of dynamite?" the kid asked the man.

"No."

"Mother give you that too?"

"Absolutely."

The kid gave the man a sour look, pushed back his coat to give a good show of his revolvers. He tapped the butts of the pistols with his fingers.

"You're funnin' me, Mister. Ought not do that. These guns are special orders. Took months just to get here. I don't wear them just for show."

"No shit?"

"You making sport of me, fella?"

"That's too much work."

"I'm fast, smart mouth. Real fast. I don't want to have to kill you."

"Only thing you're going to kill is time. Take a walk, kid."

The kid's right hand moved to draw his revolver, and he moved fast. But the man drew the kid's left revolver from his holster before the kid could clear the other, used the revolver's barrel like a club against the kid's head.

The kid dropped to the floor like a dead bird, his hat flying off.

The man laid the revolver on the bar. He looked at the bartender, pointed to his glass. "One more time."

⟨4⟩

When the drink was poured, the man put another stack of coins on the bar, strolled over to the card table carrying his drink. He said, "Name's Smith. Can I get a hand in this game?"

Quill tossed his head toward the kid on the floor.

"I think you bent the barrel on his special ordered pistol."

Smith didn't respond.

"Kind of a dangerous place to be carrying that dynamite, ain't it?"

"What dynamite?"

"That's funny, Smith," Quill said. "But not that funny."

"It's no never mind to me," Smith said.

"It ain't you we're worried about," the undertaker said. "Wouldn't take much for us all to go up."

"Guess you'll just have to be nervous," Smith said.

Quill grinned at Smith. "Hell, it ain't no never mind to me either."

Smith looked at the Indian. He hadn't even looked up from his cards. Smith said, "You the nervous type."

"Not so you could tell it," the Indian said.

"This here is McBride, but we just call him Undertaker. Chief here is Bull. I'm Trumbo Quill. I kind of keep things together around here."

"He means he runs the town and the rest of us no goods let him," Bull said.

"Something like that," Quill said. "You want to go shit, I tell you when and where and what to use to wipe your ass."

"Don't think I'll be here long enough to have to ask that permission," Smith said.

"As for me," Bull said, "I'm just passing through."

"Yeah," Quill said, "for three months now you been passing through."

"I like the cards and I like the way you run the town because you been good enough not to run me," Bull said.

Quill pushed his hat back, yelled at the bar, "Tell Payday to come out and bring a bottle of whisky."

"I'll get it," Double Shot said.

"I don't want you go get it," Quill said. "I want something good to look at. Have Payday bring it. And now."

A woman with the face of an angel, eyes as blue as a summer sky, hair the color of a brush fire, and a body that would make Jesus break the Holy Grail, came out of the back of the saloon, pushed through the beaded curtain, carrying a deck of cards and a bottle of whisky. She was wearing a fluffy white dress with blood red flowers stitched into it, had on knee high, laced, black boots. When she moved she swayed and the men watched her sway; their beady blood-shots followed her ass like a dog following a meat wagon.

Payday put the bottle next to Quill and gave the cards to McBride, the undertaker. She looked at Smith. She showed him she had all her teeth and that they were white as sugar cubes.

The Undertaker opened the deck and began to shuffle the cards.

Payday said to Smith, "Bring you a bottle, mister?"

"Bring me anything that don't kill me, Red," Smith said.

"People here call me Payday, not Red."

"That's cause they all give it up for her either in the bar or in the bed," Bull said. "She looks top notch, but she's low dollar."

Payday glared at Bull and went away. After a moment, she came back with a bottle of whisky. She put it on the table next to Smith. Smith looked at his bottle, and then he looked at Quill, and got it. The bottle Payday placed for Quill was set in such a way—behind his card hand and to the side—that Smith could see Quill's cards in the bottle's reflection. When Smith looked up, he saw Payday was looking at what he was looking at. She said, "I got a feeling today is your lucky goddamn day."

"Could be," Smith said, and pulled a cigar from his vest pocket.

"You ain't gonna light that, are you?" Undertaker asked.

"Yep," Smith said, and produced a match and struck it on his belt buckle, inches from the stick of dynamite. He puffed gently and blew smoke out of his mouth without removing the cigar.

"I think I might fold and go outside," Undertaker said.

"Go where you want to go," Smith said.

"You ain't goin' nowhere, Undertaker," Quill said. "Once you're in a game, you're in. You can fold, you want, but you'll stay sit."

Undertaker turned his eyes toward his cards, dipped his head so that the narrow brim of the stovepipe hid his eyes.

Quill twisted his mouth a moment, said, "These damn cards are no better than before." He started to pour a whisky.

Payday said, "I'll do it. That's one thing I'm paid for."

She took the bottle and dotted his glass with whisky and set the bottle back in the exact same place. Smith watched as the reflection from the cards jumped and floated in the bobbing whisky, and then the whisky went still and so did the reflection. Quill wasn't bluffing. His hand wasn't any good.

Quill said, "Think I'll fold, take Payday in the back and dip my wick."

"Not today," Payday said.

Quill turned in his chair and glared at Payday. "I don't care if you're runnin' the red river or just ain't in the mood. I say we ride a little, we ride."

"I can turn down anyone's dollar I take a mind to," Payday said. "And you're a filthy pig and I'm turning yours down."

"I never said anything about paying you," Quill said.

The fat-assed whore with the missing teeth at the next table said, "I'll do you, Quill. On the house." She got out of the buckskinned man's lap and moved toward him.

Quill said, "I don't fuck goats."

This stopped the fat whore as surely as a punch in the head. She went back and sat down in a chair at the table with the buckskinners. She didn't look at Quill. She didn't look at the men at the table. The buckskin-dressed man whose lap she had been sitting in tried to encourage her with a smile, but his scattering of teeth didn't warm her. She continued to stay where she was.

Quill stood up, grabbed Payday's arm, "Come on," he said.

"Let go of me, you pig."

Quill didn't let go.

Payday shot a glance at Smith. He looked at her, but there was nothing in his face that gave her comfort. She looked at the undertaker. He picked up his cards and shuffled them in his hands with a sound like startled quail flying from a bush. His skin turned red.

She didn't bother looking at Bull.

Quill pulled her across the floor and through the beaded curtain, and just before they went through, she reached for his gun, and almost had it when Quill grabbed her hand and pushed it aside, said, "No you don't. I know what you can do with that and you ain't gonna do nothin'."

Quill shoved her through the curtain and followed. A moment later there was a sound of a struggle, then a grunt. This was followed by, "You little whore," and then there was the sound of Quill forcing her upstairs, and then the floor creaked, and then there was a yelp and the sound of a struggle, and then something hit the floor.

A moment later, the struggle started all over again. Bull said, "I reckon he's havin' seconds."

The sleeping man at the nearby table hadn't flexed a muscle and now he was snoring.

(5)

The fat saloon girl came over and said to Smith. "You look like a nice man. Won't you help her?"

"I'm not nice," Smith said. "Leave me out of it. I learned a long time ago to mind my own business."

The saloon girl looked around the room in desperation. No takers. She went back and sat down and cried almost silently. Upstairs, the screams increased and so did the blows. Finally, Bull said, "I'm gonna get in line, see if there's anything left."

"Not today," Smith said.

"What?"

Smith reached inside his coat and took out a rolled piece of paper, put it on the table and unrolled it, smoothed it with his palm. It was a crude drawing of Bull. It was a wanted poster. Smith tapped his finger against it, said, "That's you."

"That could be any Indian with a bowler hat," Bull said.

"That's you. It even says Bull. How many Bulls are there that look like you and wear a bowler hat?"

Bull grinned. "I look a lot better in person, don't you think?"

"Yeah, but there's the smell."

"I get lonely on the plains. The smell attracts buffalo, and you know what they say; 'it's all pink on the inside.'"

"And this says Wanted Dead or Alive."

Bull pushed his chair back, stood up and said, "Well, it won't be alive."

"I prefer it that way. Less stops for pee breaks."

"You got to make me dead first."

Bull flipped open his coat to give him freer access to the holstered sawed-off. The buckskinners and the saloon girl at the table behind them moved away quickly. Gun like that could take out a room.

Bull grinned and gently touched the sawed off stock of the shotgun. "I ain't no punk kid."

Before the words were fully out of his mouth, Smith drew.

No one really saw it.

There was a blur and there was a noise, and the next thing they realized, the back of Bull's head was decorating the wall and Bull was lying on the floor in a heap, pissing himself. The echo of the shot hung in the air.

The sleeping man at the nearby table still hadn't moved a muscle and he was still snoring.

Smith glanced at Undertaker.

"Okay with me," said Undertaker holding up his hands, "it's good business."

"You don't get this one," Smith said. "Reward money."

"Just saying I understand commerce when I see it, mine or someone else's."

Smith put the revolver away and folded up his wanted poster and put it inside his coat pocket. Upstairs Quill yelled, "I'll cut your face off, whore."

"She needs help, you know," Undertaker said, lifting his head to the upper floor.

"Then go help her."

Smith grabbed Bull by one of his heels and pulled him across the floor and through the bat wings. Double Shot came out behind him.

"Someone ought to help that girl."

"You got a bone in your leg," Smith said. "You can walk. Go help her you want to."

Double Shot looked down at the board walk.

Smith tossed Bull over the horse next to his at the hitching post.

"Mister," Double Shot said, "that ain't Bull's horse. That one belongs to Quill."

"Tell him life is full of all manner of little disappointments."

Smith got on his horse while holding the reins of the other, started trotting down the street, Quill's horse in tow, carrying Bull's body.

(6)

Inside the saloon the beaded curtain parted, and out stumbled Payday. She had her hand over the side of her face covering her eye. Blood leaked through her fingers. Her hair was loose and cascaded across her back and shoulders and across her cheek like lava flowing. At first glance, it looked as if the red flowers on her dress had multiplied, but they were not in the shapes of flowers, they were crimson splotches and some of them were spreading. She staggered. She turned. Her hand slipped down from her face. There was a lot of blood and a lot of wound. She collapsed to the floor with a loud thud.

The fat saloon girl jumped up and ran over to the sleeping man and grabbed his shoulder and shook him. "Doc, for God's sake, wake up. Payday's been hurt."

Doc didn't move.

The saloon girl shook him harder. "Quill's done messed her up bad."

Doc stirred, causing the whisky bottle he had been clutching to fall and hit the floor. He said, "What now?"

"Payday. She's been hurt by Quill. Doc. Come on. You got to help."

Doc got up and steadied his hand on the back of the chair for support. The saloon girl picked up his black bag, started pushing Doc toward Payday. At that moment, Quill came through the beaded curtain buttoning up his pants. He took a look at Payday on the floor, went over to the bar and saw that Double Shot was standing just outside of the bat wings. "Hey, Double Shot. Get your ass in here. I need a drink."

Double Shot rushed inside, said, "Mister Quill."

"Shut up," Quill said. He turned and put his back against the bar. The doctor was on his knees beside the unconscious Payday, looking her over. Quill said, "Fix her up so she lives, we'll put a bag over her head and give her away free to sell beer."

"Mr. Quill," Double Shot said.

"What, goddamnit!"

"The stranger… He killed Bull and put him on your horse and took off."

Quill whirled to look at Double Shot. "What?"

"That's right, took your horse."

"Damnit. Why didn't you tell me, you asshole? Hand me that Winchester from under the bar, the long barrel one."

Double Shot bent down and got it and gave it to Quill.

The doctor, still wobbling, looked up and saw Quill, said, "What happened? What did you do, Quill?"

"I was you," Quill said, moving toward the swinging doors, "I wouldn't concern myself with it."

Quill ran outside and looked up the street and cocked the Winchester. He saw Smith not too far away, in no hurry, trotting along on his horse, leading Quill's horse with Bull lying across it. Bull was dripping blood onto the sandy street. Quill raised the Winchester and fired.

The shot hit Smith's horse smooth in the ass, a blue whistler that went in deep and killed the beast. As it fell, quivering, it tossed Smith into the dirt. Smith, tumbled and rolled to his feet, and when he came up, he had both pistols in his hands, his cigar still clenched in his teeth. Quill's horse sprinted wildly away, tearing down the street, heading for the unknown, Bull on board.

Smith sauntered up the street, back toward the saloon, holding both pistols, puffing at his cigar, the smoke trailing behind him. "I liked that horse," he said to no one in particular.

Smith saw Quill raising the Winchester again, and snapped off a shot. It hit the saloon wall next to Quill, frayed the wood there, knocking splinters back into Quill's cheek. Another shot cracked the wood, and Quill ducked back inside the saloon faster than a jack rabbit diving down a hole.

A moment passed, no longer than the time it would take a cricket to jump, and Quill came out again, aimed the Winchester at Smith and fired. Smith winced slightly and his cigar went from one side of his mouth to the other, but his teeth saved it. Smith fired again, and this time his shot was good. It hit Quill in the side, low. Quill went to one knee, raised the rifle and shot back. The bullet plucked at Smith's shirt collar, tore on through, went spinning down the street and fell into the dust.

Smith put his pistols in their holsters with a slick spinning move, pulled the stick of dynamite out of his belt and touched the wick to the tip of his cigar. There was a hissss like an angry snake as the dynamite lit. Smith was close now, and Quill was firing steadily, but there wasn't a good aim in the bunch. The shots fluttered around Smith's head and body like bees.

Smith pulled the dynamite back to throw it, and as he did he noticed something too late. The wick. The goddamn wick.

"Too short," Smith said aloud, with no more surprise than if he had discovered a fly on his dinner plate. Before he could throw it, the dynamite went off, and when it did, the blast was so vicious it set the saddle bag of dynamite on the dead horse behind him off, and then there was one hell of an explosion. Smith and horsemeat went in all directions. The remains of his revolvers clattered against the buildings on either side of the street, and his clothes were coasted on the wind. Blood and bones splattered and stuck to the clapboard sidings. Windows blew out of businesses, dust stirred up and whirled about like a little tornado. A concho came down on the boardwalk in front of the saloon. Most of the saddle that had been on Smith's horse went sliding up to the livery.

When what was left of Smith and his horse settled, and the dust settled too. People came out of the saloon and buildings along the sun-hot street and looked where Smith had stood. Kids stole pieces of his shirt and pants, and one put on his smoking, hole-pocked hat and ran away with it.

Quill, standing outside the saloon. He laid the barrel of the Winchester against his shoulder, turned to Double Shot, who had exited to stand on the boardwalk with an expression like a steer that had just been hit with a hammer.

Double Shot said, "You hurt her bad, Quill. You shouldn't have."

Quill not paying attention, pointed the Winchester in the direction where Smith had stood before the explosion, said, "That Smith fella, he ought to have got someone with a better eye for measurement to trim his wicks."

PART TWO:

The Devil Be Damned

The worst thing about death must be the first night.
JOSE RAMÓN JIMÉNEZ

⟨1⟩

This saloon was nowhere near Falling Rock. It was a large and fine establishment with a big ass mirror and shiny beer taps and rows of shimmering bottles of whisky and liquors in all the colors of the rainbow and a long bar with a solid gold foot rest. It was warm inside, even steamy, and though it was a neat bar, there was a smell about the place that couldn't quite be identified. It could be said to be somewhere between something dead gone to rot, fear sweat, and aging horse shit. Breathing the air was akin to swallowing flannel and tasting burnt matches. The floor was Arab tile, and it depicted all manner of sexual positions between men and women, and men and men, and women and women, and beasts and men, and beasts and beasts, and some funny looking guy doing something to a knot hole in a big oak tree.

Behind the bar, a snappy looking bartender that looked to be quite proud of himself, was rubbing down the bar with a rag that looked as if he had wiped his ass on it. In spite of that, the bar appeared clean and shiny. The bartender's eyebrows were amazingly arched, and his hair was slicked down tighter than the skin on a drum, parted in the center. He had the kind of mouth that looked as if a hook belonged in it. His cheek bones were so sharp you could open mail with them. He was wearing a white shirt with red stripes and silver studs in the button holes and elbow garters dark as doom. Fat black flies hovered over his head as if it were a dung pile. They buzzed so loudly they almost hurt the ears. Sometimes it sounded as if they might be whispering words, words Smith couldn't quite hear, but there was something about the sound that was vulgar. As the bartender moved along the bar, a limp was slightly noticeable.

Two Mohawk Indians with their hair cut in long, bushy bands across their skulls, their bodies peppered with holes, wearing only breech cloths, were leaning on the bar, guzzling whisky from fly-swarmed bottles. One lifted his leg to fart, and when he did a flame jumped out from under his breech cloth. The cloth fluttered in the air, crackled a little and flared sparks. It sparked a short-lived blaze, then lay down on his ass again, once again flameless.

"Bad whisky?" said the other.

"Bad whisky," said the farter.

There were lots of tables in the room. At one of them, a Roman soldier removed his helmet, poured blood out of it, onto the tile, splattering onto his sandals. A six-legged yellow dog came in quickly and began to lick it up. The Roman's head leaked blood through his hair and onto his face. A black cat jumped up on his knee and reared up on its hind legs and licked his blood-stained face, and he let it.

Another man, dressed like a miner, covered in dust, was sitting in a chair nearby, headless. He supported his shaggy-haired, bearded head on his knee with one dirty hand, like it was a hat he was soon to wear. He took a glass of liquor and poured it into the head's mouth. The rotgut ran out of the stump of its neck and gathered on the miner's knee, drenching his pants. The drinking head smacked its lips and licked the air with its tongue, closed its eyes as if to sleep.

And there was Bull. He was the only one sitting at a table alone, drinking from a dirty glass. Flies were on the wound in his forehead. One of the flies crawled into the hole, came out quick, buzzing its wings as if to say: "Hey guys, come on, you got to see this," and then the fly scuttled back into the bullet puncture and out of sight. The back of Bull's head, where the bullet came out, had a huge gap of exploded flesh and bone. Brains dripped out of the back of his skull like spoiled oatmeal.

Across the way, a door burst open and a wheelbarrow was taxied through. Pushing it was a muscular, young, blonde woman wearing only a sweat-wet strip of black cloth between her legs. He bare breasts swung and crashed together like oily bowling balls. The little bit of cloth she wore was fastened so tight when she walked it looked as if her buttocks were polishing a pearl. She was tanned and tattooed with snakes and spiders across her back and belly, and the tattoos crawled.

In the wheelbarrows were steaming, bloody, body parts with pieces of clothing dotted throughout. There was a black hat resting on top of the pile of guts, brains and bone. Flies flocked to this so enthusiastically and so loudly, they sounded like lumberjacks working saws.

The blonde tipped the wheelbarrow and the mess splattered onto the floor, ran a little, and then heaped up. The pile smoked and the haze of the smoke covered the mess. Then something rose up through the smoke. Guts whipped in the air like searching, elongated fingers, and then bone fragments in the wheelbarrow clicked together like dice being shook, rapidly formed a skeleton. The flesh quivered and climbed across the bones, and the guts crawled in through holes in the flesh, and the holes sealed up. Scraps of cloth gathered up and bound together, and soon the body was covered in shirt and pants and boots and vest and a long black coat. The man took a deep breath and his eyes popped open. He picked up his hat and put it on his head carefully.

He walked slowly to the bar, leaned on it, put a foot on the boot rest and looked in the mirror.

Good as new, Smith thought. Well, almost good as new.

His skin still showed rips, but the rips were healing. The mustache was gone, and his hat had holes in it. As he watched, the holes in his hat filled in.

Smith coughed out some dust and gun powder and dynamite wrappings, turned and watched the blonde's ass as she took the wheelbarrow by its handles, swung her slick, round buttocks through the open door and out of sight, still polishing that pearl.

The door closed silently behind her, swooshing into the bar an aroma of sex and sweat and something dead.

(2)

The bartender came down the bar still wiping. When he was in front of Smith, he said: "She, meaning the sweaty little thing with the wheelbarrow, had to take that hat from a kid. He thought a crow took it off his head, but it was her. She thought you might want it back. How are you?"

"A little dazed," Smith said.

"Ears ringing?"

"A bit."

"It'll pass quickly."

"That's good."

"Drink?" the bartender asked, but he was already pouring whisky from a bottle into a small glass that Smith hadn't noticed a moment before. "On the house."

"Don't mind if I do," Smith said, examining himself in the mirror. "I look like me, but not exactly."

"It never comes together just right. I can't tell you how many times we've forgotten to put assholes back in. Really, it doesn't matter that much, but it's sort of an aesthetic thing, you know."

"I would think it would matter a lot."

"Suppose you're right. It matters. But here's the thing, you look younger."

Smith realized his ears were no longer ringing. In fact, he felt really good.

When he looked in the mirror again, he noticed his face had become smooth; he did look younger. Ten years younger. Less leathery, and less worn. He took the drink and swallowed it with one gulp.

"Another?" the bartender asked, already pouring.

Smith took it, glanced at the mirror again. But this time, there was no reflection. Instead his life was reflected there, working in reverse. There was the gunfight with Quill, the stupidity of the short fuse on the dynamite, and Smith started thinking maybe he had done it intentionally.

Maybe the totality of his life was too heavy, why else would he do such a dumb thing? And then there was the red-headed woman, what did they call her? Payday. That was it. He could see her in the mirror, what had been done to her face. And so it went, his life playing in reverse, and Smith thought that when it was all added up, it didn't amount to much, unless you were scoring for murder and mayhem. On backwards his life fled, and it was full of gunfire and knifings and dying and disappointment and frequent bad fashion, including a temporary trend toward chaps and boots with metal-tipped toes.

The bartender stepped into Smith's line of vision, and smiled. It was a big smile, and Smith thought there were more teeth there than there should have been, and for a moment, he thought he saw something move in the bartender's eyes, and then he was certain of it. The eyes leaped with images of flames and murder and war. It was as if he were looking through little peep holes in time and space. Soldiers moved across the surface of the eyes, and there were bursts of gunfire in the irises, and faintly Smith thought he heard voices and screams. Smith felt hypnotized as he watched all manner of history unfold across and within the bartender's peepers, and all of what he saw was bad and rotten and made him wish for the survival of the "lesser" species and the extermination of humanity, which appeared to have nothing human about it. He concluded the short fuse on the dynamite had been a good idea, and his only wish was that the explosion could have wiped all of humanity off the globe, along with him.

The bartender moved slightly, and the last thing Smith saw in his eyes was the falling of a guillotine. Smith was looking at the mirror again. It was just a mirror. Smith said, "That's some mirror you got."

"I like it," the bartender said.

Smith discovered his glass had been filled again. He tossed the whisky down. It really was awful stuff. "This tastes awful," he said.

"You're tellin' me. And you do not want to know what it's made out of. Another?"

Smith looked at his glass. "No. I think that will hold me."

"Sure?"

"Oh, what the hell? Hit me again."

The bartender poured Smith another glass. Smith said, "I got a feeling you know who I am."

"Smith," the bartender said.

"And what's your name?"

"Oh, I have a variety, but you can call me Snappy."

"I take it this isn't Wyoming anymore."

"Nope."

Smith picked up the glass of whisky, turned and leaned his back on the bar, looked at the crowd behind him. Their reflections had not been available in the mirror. Sitting nearby was Bull, swarmed with flies. As Smith watched, the number thirteen appeared out of nowhere, pinned to Bull's shirt. In fact, now everyone wore the number thirteen. Some of the men and women were bare-chested, and the number had been pinned to them with huge safety pins, right through the flesh on their chests.

A large metal-studded door opposite the one through which Smith had entered, swung open with a sound like bones being pulled loose from flesh. Then came screams and moans and wails and all manner of begging for mercy, and then there were flashes of fire. Smith turned and looked into the room and saw people with meat hooks through their necks swing by. The smell of burning flesh was intense. He hated that it reminded him of good barbecue.

The people on hooks dangled along as if on a carousel, and then the carousel stopped, and Smith could see one of the smoking bodies was alive with worms, and they were crawling in and out of holes like fingers poking through fingerless gloves.

Snappy called out, "Thirteen, you're next."

Bull stood up. He had a mug of beer in his hand.

Smith said without turning to look at Snappy, "They're all thirteen."

"They know who's who."

"Then why the number?"

"Here, that sort of thing works quite well, and the number, well, it's also very appropriate. This isn't exactly a place of good luck, if you know what I mean."

Bull tipped his bowler at Smith, began walking toward the open flame-kissed door, the back of his head dripping blood and brains. He paused and looked back at Smith.

"Maybe we should have helped that girl."

"Maybe we should have done a lot of things," Smith said.

"Good point," Bull said, and moved closer to the door. A long goo-dripping tentacle appeared amidst the flames, reached out, wrapped around Bull and squeezed him until his eyes popped out on the tendons and hung down on his cheeks, then it pulled him into the flaming room and the door slammed shut, causing Bull's bowler to fly off and roll back into the room on its rim. It fell on its crown and lay at Smith's feet.

Smith nudged it with the toe of his boot.

"Now I know where I am," he said.

(3)

Smith turned to look at the bartender, said, "Now I know who you are."

"Flattered to be recognized, and I'm all about flattery, you know?"

"What now? Do I take a number?"

"Not yet. And if you want to keep from taking a number, want to stay out of there," Snappy said pointing at the big door through which Bull had exited, "then you might want to listen to a little proposition I have for you."

"I'm all ears."

"It's right down your alley."

"Said I was listening."

Snappy nodded, reached up to scratch behind his ear, and then placed both hands on the bar. Smith looked at them. For the first time, he noticed that Snappy's fingers were a little long and the nails were long too, and though he had seemed immaculate before, now his fingers looked grungy, and there was certainly something dark under the nails.

"Some of my hired help have gotten a little too big for their britches; think they don't have to listen to me anymore. They're up there," Snappy jerked a thumb toward the ceiling, "causing trouble, and that twists my multiple sets of genitalia into an uncomfortable knot, that's what I'm telling you."

"Multiple sets?"

"I have more than one pecker, and more than one set of apples. Got me?"

"That must require special pants."

"Tell me about it."

"Thing throws me is, I thought you were all about trouble. I mean, after all, you're...well, you know who you are. Why would you care about someone causing trouble."

"Not this kind of trouble. I got a wild one on the loose, messing with things he doesn't have a right to bother with. No respect for authority, and I'm about being obeyed more than I'm about being right or wrong. And, in a way, I'm mostly wrong. Anyway, this rogue, he was a pretty good right-hand man for a while, but now he's decided he wants to run things. He's taken something that doesn't belong to me. Something even I don't mess with, and I don't like it even a little bit. That's where you come in."

"Could that happen?" Smith said. "Him running things? I mean, is that possible? After all, you're... You."

"I know who I am. Okay?"

"Sure."

"It's more complex than that. Me and him... We don't say his name here. Same way we don't say my true name. Just not done. Bad form. But the bottom line is, there are folks on earth who don't think we're very good for mankind, and you know, they're right. That's my job. That's the job I was given, and I do it to the best of my ability. I've never understood how humans can worship... Well, you know. HIM. He's the one gave me my job. He could have just given everyone a good life to begin with, but no, he had to put me in charge of giving you people problems, offering you alternatives, so to speak, and then in the end, he judges you. It's just a big game, you know."

"I've often thought that," Smith said.

"In his own way, he's as mean as I am. Meaner."

"I'll buy that," Smith said.

"But the bottom line is this: The one up there, and I don't mean way up there, but, you know, on earth, and we'll use one of his names that can be used, Zelzarda, if he gets his hands on the switch, there will be real chaos."

"You mean he could run the whole kit and kaboodle?"

"Yep."

"Maybe I should kick in with him."

Snappy grinned his too many teeth. "We can call the whole thing off, and you can go through that door, assisted by a tentacle."

"Just kidding," Smith said. "But this all sounds a little over my head. I'm just a bounty hunter."

"You want to hear me out, or not?"

"Shoot."

"Let's keep it simple for you. There's a place on earth where all the configuration points of the universe come together. You just came from that place."

"Falling Rock?"

"Yep."

"I'll be damned."

"That part is still under consideration. It depends on you."

"I'm really listening."

"There's a place there like a gate, and on the other side of the gate are a group we call The Old Ones. Right timing, right spells, they can come through. No more heaven and hell as we know it. No more balance. Zelzarda wants to open that gate. If he brings The Old Ones through, he'll rule The Old Ones, which means he'll rule chaos."

"I thought the whole point of chaos was that it was unruly."

Snappy nodded. "But, when Zelzarda wants something done, it will be done. He will be king of both hell and heaven. But, as you said, rule is a general word. It'll be a mess. I like things the way they are. This way me and the other guy compete, we have a little fun, we see who wins one day, who wins the next. If The Old Ones take over, I won't be in such a good position, and neither will the other guy. You see where I'm going with this?"

"I think so."

"What I want you to do is go up there and kick his ass. Put his candle out. Stop the spell and The Old Ones. Kill the disloyal bastard… Oh, and one more thing. Remember, he will find a host to take human form. The host will be someone who gives Zelzarda his soul. That is part of the spell. He must have a willing soul to start the spell."

"That's it?"

"That's the start. It's like this. The spell is words of a sort. Hieroglyphics comes closer to a description. Shapes. Figures. Nasty little bastards left on this world by The Old Ones. Words that escaped from the Necronomicon."

"The what?"

"It's a book of dark spells."

"Words escaped from the book?"

"That's exactly what happened. The words are like dark little bugs and they left the book. Ran off… Don't worry. You don't have to understand all of this. Just do what I tell you. The key to everything is in a book. You see those bad old words were mine. I had them in a special box, tucked away, and Zelzarda stole the box."

"You should have been more careful with that box."

Snappy frowned. "You aren't pushing me, are you?"

Smith shook his head.

"You have one night and three days earth time. Summer solstice is June 21. Big day for folks in my trade. Supernatural powers at their peak, all that sort of business."

"Can I do it in three days?"

"And one night," Snappy said.

"All right. Can I do it in one night and three days?"

"I don't know. Can you? I'll tell you this. You can either give it a try or stay here, or worse yet, Zelzarda wins and—"

"Would I really be worse off?"

"I'm going to vote, yes. You have skills, and you do this for me, for the world, for the universe, then I'll see what I can do for you."

"Maybe I can empty the trash for you."

"Or, you can go through that door."

"Good point," Smith said.

"A year has passed since you been up there."

"A year."

"Time moves different in the netherworld. But up there, when you get there, three days is three days."

"And there's that one night," Smith said.

Snappy nodded. "And the one night."

"Kind of waited until the last minute, didn't you?"

"Waited until the time was right. All the configurations and the like."

"I don't mean to be rude, but, you're...you know."

"I told you, I know quite well who I am."

"So, why—"

"—don't I go get him myself?"

"Exactly."

"You're walking on thin ice, Smith. You're talking yourself out of a job. I don't do that kind of dirty work. That's why I've got you. For me to do it personally, bad form. Puts me on Zelzarda's level."

"Oh."

"It's either go back and do what I ask, or—"

Snappy waved a hand and the big door opened and flames licked out. Smith could see Bull's nude body on a hook. Bull swung by. His testicles were being gnawed by creatures that looked somewhere between bumble bees and bats. Flames licked out of the hollows of his eyes. Bull was screaming like a little girl with a thorn in her foot.

"It never stops," Snappy said. "Things grow back, and things get gnawed off again. Eyes come back, they get burned out again. There are all manner of creative ideas here."

"All right then, I'm riding for the brand," Smith said.

The door slammed shut, leaving an intense whiff of sulfur and a stench of burning flesh in the air.

"I thought you might be. You're going to need a little more than a stick of dynamite for this job."

(4)

Snappy's hands hardly moved, or at least not so you could see them, and in the next instant he had a .45 revolver in each one. He placed the revolvers on the bar. The metal was ebony and the butts were black pearl with tiny, red, flame-lick designs.

Smith picked them up, gave them a once over. When he touched them, they seemed to grow into his hands. It was an eerie feeling. He put them down without problem, picked them up again. Same sensation. He thumbed one of the hammers back. The action was smooth. He closed down the hammer and put the gun on the bar.

"Nice."

"They shoot as smooth as they feel," Snappy said.

"Guns made here?" Smith asked.

"Course not," Snappy said. "Samuel Colt. We can't improve on that. We give them a little rub with goat oil and our special formula, that way they really feel good in the hands. But, Colt, he can't be beat for balance, wear and aim. The ammunition is silver. A lot of folk of my kind don't like it. It also has some spells said over it."

"What about you and silver?"

"Not a favorite here either, but, if I got to deal with it, I can. I mean, after all, I am who I am. Zelzarda, not so much. At least not yet. But if he gets what he wants, and The Old Ones come through, he'll be the most powerful creature in the universe that ever was or ever will be."

Snappy pulled a double holster gun belt out of thin air, plopped it on the bar. There's only one bullet in the belt.

"Can't do much with one bullet," Smith said.

Snappy picked up the belt and pulled out the single bullet. The instant he did, the bullet loops filled up completely. "You never get down to your last bullet, long as you're wearing this."

"I'll be damned."

"I advise you to find another expression," Snappy said.

Snappy swung fancy saddle bags onto the bar, black with silver studs on them. He opened one of the bags and took out a stick of dynamite. "And you still got your trademark, Smith. But, the wicks are longer, and you got to be careful. You go back, you'll be flesh and blood again. I don't want you blowing yourself up before the job is done. Last, but not least, how about a little posse."

"Well, it has been awhile," Smith said, pushing his hat back on his head.

"Posse, Smith. Posse. Pay attention."

"Oh… No thanks. I work alone."

"You haven't always worked alone."

"If you mean the war, riding for Quantrail. I'm not proud of that."

"So, you've gained a bit of conscience."

"Quite recently, I might add."

"Since you've been here."

"Absolutely."

"That's fear you're feeling, not conscience. I don't believe you're one bit different."

"I got three days, and that's it, I better get started," Smith said.

"Sure you don't want that posse?"

"Sure."

"Suit yourself. Change your mind—" Snappy fanned a small stack of playing cards out of nowhere, spread them on the bar. On the face of the cards were portraits. "These are your aces in the hole." Snappy pulled the cards together lightly and decked them and slipped them into Smith's coat pocket. "If you need them, they'll be there. And remember, up there, things have changed."

The door through which Smith entered flung open and the near naked blonde came in with a pitchfork stuck in the ass of a short, uniformed man wearing a cocked hat with his hand inside his coat. He was babbling in French. The number thirteen suddenly appeared on his uniform. The door on the far side flung open and a tentacle reached all the way across the room and grabbed the man around the head and jerked him into the flames and the door slammed shut, coughing out fire around the edges.

"That was quick," Smith said, watching the blonde disappear back through the door which remained open.

"French," Snappy said. "No waiting." Snappy poured Smith another drink. "One for the road."

Smith drank it.

Snappy said, "All right, it's time. Don't fail."

"When I ride for the brand, I ride for the brand. I do the job as best I can."

"We'll see," Snappy said.

"And since I assume I'm riding for the brand, what will I be riding? My horse got blown up."

"That was your doing."

"Still, no pony."

"I will provide, of course."

And then Smith, and everything he wore, the saddle bags included, came apart and turned into a million little brown moths that fled through the open door and up a long dark tunnel that quit being dark suddenly and filled with a burning light.

PART THREE:

Riding for the Brand

What we call destiny is truly our character,
and that character can be altered.
ANAIS NIN

⟨1⟩

That night the Sundown Saloon in Falling Rock was loud with laughter and yelling and gunfire from drunks. Upstairs in the saloon was another sound, grunting and panting, and a noise that sounded like a goat.

"Louder, bitch. Like the goat you are."

The woman beneath Quill was the saloon girl he not so long ago called a goat, and now he was making her sound like one. The sound was weak, and Quill laughed as he plunged into her. The girl looked bored, but she was making with the goat sounds, thinking: It's a living. She turned her head and watched a slow-moving moth crawl across the window pane.

Outside the saloon, descending from the bell tower across the street, came a horde of bats. They knotted together and plunged for the roof of the saloon, and just before they hit, they become a projectile of black smoke. When the smoke struck, shingles snapped, and the roof absorbed the smoke.

In the room upstairs, where Quill was riding the woman who was bleating like a goat, the smoke sifted through the cracks in the wood overhead and gathered in a wad of shadow and floated down in a funnel shape toward Quill's open, heavy-breathing mouth. The smoke had red sparkles of fire in it, and the red sparkles made shapes. They crackled and hissed as they entered Quill's mouth.

The woman saw it first, stopped bleating, tried to roll out from under Quill, but he was too heavy, too strong.

The shadow went down deep into Quill's mouth, and inside Quill's head he heard a voice say: "Time to collect."

The saloon girl screamed and shoved Quill off of her and darted naked for the door, threw it open, ran out on the landing, screeching.

Quill stretched his neck, and his eyes rolled, and his back cracked like someone popping a bull whip. He stood up in the middle of the bed, his arms stretched out. Wings tore out of his back full born and vulture black. The ripping of his skin was akin to the sound of rotten flannel being torn. The huge wings fanned the air. Quill's face knotted up as if infected with small pox, and his mouth became wide, his cheek bones sharp, his skin the texture of old leather. As he stood on the bed, his weight collapsed it. Now his toes lengthened and bunched over one another and became tight and hard—hooves. There was very little left that was recognizable as Quill. The monster watched his fingers grow long and the nails grow long as well, hook into claws. He clicked his claws together and smiled his many, pointed teeth at nothing. The demon was inside of him. Quill could only faintly remember who he truly was. All that remained of him was the bad.

{2}

Downstairs the saloon girl was yelling and pointing upstairs, but the men in the room were focused on her nudity, and for that matter, so were the women. There was a lot of meat on her, and it was moving all over, like a bowl of pudding being shaken. Then there came a roar from upstairs, and the landing shook, and something dark leaped off of it.

Wings snapped in the air, and then Quill, or what had once been Quill, dove down from the ceiling and into their midst. His first victim was the saloon girl. He snatched her head off the way a mean child might knock off the head of a dandelion with a stick. Her neck pumped blood and her big body hit the floor like a dropped cannonball.

Someone yelled out. "He ain't got no drawers on," as if this was the oddest thing about him.

In the next instant, there was a mass run for the door. The cocky kid who had challenged Smith was the first one out the door, followed by the bartender, Double Shot, and Undertaker. Doc, who usually graced a chair in the saloon, was in a ditch outside of town, sleeping one off. It was his lucky day.

The beating of Quill's wings filled the air along with the sound of his great claws swishing, the snapping of his jaws, the gnashing of his teeth, and the bellowing of the doomed.

Recuperating in Doc's office down the street, Payday heard the noise. She got up from the cot, wrapped the sheet around her naked body and looked out the window with her one good eye, saw something winged and horrible blast through the bat wings of the saloon and take to the sky, dragging an unfortunate man with it. The thing took him high up, out of Payday's sight, and then let him go. The man fell into the street with a splat, his insides flying out and in all directions.

"Goddamn," Payday said.

She quickly dressed, called for Doc, looked about. He was nowhere to be seen. The street was filled with screaming, and Payday paused long enough to glance out the window again.

Mayhem. People were rushing about, and the winged horror was having at them, tooth and nail. Diving down, jerking limbs and heads off, slashing at them, playing with them. The dirt in the street looked as damp as if it had just received an evening rain; the moonlight flicked wetly in the slick dark pools of blood.

Okay, Payday thought, I've seen enough.

Just before she started out the back door, she glanced at her reflection in a dark mirror. The bandage over her torn eye had begun to spot with blood.

When Quill finished, many had escaped, but that didn't matter. He needed an army, and though they didn't know it yet, the escapees were it. He picked up the head of one of the dead men and walked awkwardly on his hooves toward the saloon. When he walked, he made a sound like something bound together with ancient canvas. His hooves clattered when he climbed on the boardwalk, and as he entered the saloon. He sat the head on the table and took a chair, which almost didn't hold his weight. He clawed the top of the decapitated head open, and with his talons, began to scoop out the brains, which he ate ravenously.

But he chewed with his mouth closed. That was in the back of his mind. When you eat, keep your mouth closed. His mother had taught him manners. That part of him that was Quill, remembered that.

The saloon filled with flies, and then a cold wind blew down the street and into the saloon and blew out the lamps.

The thing that was now Quill ate in the dark.

(3)

Some miles away from Falling Rock, a full year later, the darkness was split by light oozing between the weathered boards of a barricaded, abandoned mine shaft. The sound of hoof beats could be heard, growing louder and louder in the tunnel. The light expanded, and then the boards covering the shaft burst apart, cracking like thunder, tossing the rotting lumber too and fro.

A huge horse, seventeen hands high, leaped out of the shaft, a horse so dark it could almost be mistaken for a shadow. On its back, seated on a saddle as dark as spit-polished death, dressed in his black attire, but looking sharper and fresher than before, was Smith. The horse reared up so that it framed itself and Smith against the moon. Its forelegs pawed at the air. The light in the tunnel went out and there was a puff of smoke and a blast of heat at Smith's back and then there was just the cool air of the night. In the distance, coyotes howled.

As the horse dropped its front legs to earth, Snappy's voice filled Smith's head: "His name is Shadow. He can run all day and he can run all night, never tires. Take note that much time has passed since you were blown to hell, since your return. And one more thing, beware of the long dark night and the two moons."

"Can you hear me, Snappy," Smith said to the darkness.

"I hear you," said the voice in his head. It was Snappy, of course.

"Why don't you cut the mumbo jumbo crap and just talk straight?"

"Mumbo jumbo is how it's done," Snappy's voice said. "We have our rules. They may not make sense to you, but we move in mysterious ways. Last thing I tell you is this. I can get you in, but I can't get you out. It's on you."

"What?" Smith said.

But the voice was gone, and Smith knew that from here on out he was on his own.

Smith rode down a long trail and onto the main road, and as he went past the sign that read Falling Rock, the air shimmered blue and there was a swishing sound behind him. When he turned in the saddle to look, the blue light was dying, and an instant later it was gone.

Smith rode back to the sign, but found he and Shadow could proceed no further. There was an invisible barrier.

"That's what he meant about getting me in, but not getting me out," Smith said, leaning down to pat the side of Shadow's huge head.

Smith wheeled the horse and began riding slowly along the road. He had not gone far, when he saw a light in the distance. He could hear singing; a chorus of voices. He got off Shadow and led the horse behind him. As he neared the sound, he could see shapes around a camp fire, the source of the light. Men. Cowboys. They had their backs to him and were singing songs together. They were really bad at it, like bull frogs in pain.

Smith kept leading Shadow, and pretty soon he could make out the shapes of their horses in the shadows beyond. Most importantly, he could smell coffee.

As Smith came closer, the song ended and was followed by a chuckle from the cowboys. He saw there was a mass of cowboys around the fire. He wasn't sure how many exactly, but a lot. One of them was reaching for the coffee pot on the fire. The cowboy picked it up, and when he did, his arm fell off and the coffee fell with it.

When the cowboy jumped back in surprise, the others began laughing. Angry, the cowboy turned sideways, and in the firelight Smith got a good look at him. The look made Smith freeze.

The cowboy's face was as much bone as flesh, the teeth showing on one side of his mouth where the skin was gone, his eye on that side like a marble in a hole. His jaw was oddly long, as if it had been stretched. The rest of him was ragged clothes and ragged flesh. His now empty sleeve flapped in the wind.

The Lost Arm Cowboy looked directly at one of the others in the circle, said, "You think that's pretty funny, don't you Zeke?"

Just as he finished speaking, his jaw swung half open, as if on a hinge. A tooth popped out, showed as a dark dot in the firelight, and then dropped out of sight. The cowboy grabbed his jaw and tried to push it back into position, but it wouldn't snap back into place. It just hung there. The cowboy made a noise akin to: "Fug."

The other cowboys really laughed this time. The one called Zeke, said, "You sure are funny, Slim. What's left of you, I mean."

That got another round of laughter.

Smith stood still. He could see the other cowboys as they turned from their sitting positions on the ground to look at Slim and his dangling jaw. They too had abnormally long jaws and their features had a compressed look. Their ears seemed too long and their eyes too deep. Rotating on a spit over the fire was the cooking head of a child.

"Shit," Smith said.

Then Smith took note of what Shadow was paying attention to. The horses. They were mostly thin skin stretched over bones, and raw muscle was visible where patches of flesh had rotted away. They had elongated faces, the snouts narrow, as if designed to poke comfortably into pickle jars. When they stirred you could hear their leathery hides cracking and creaking. The wind carried a stench that no one would mistake for petunias.

Shadow snorted.

The cowboys jumped to their feet and looked in Smith and Shadow's direction.

"Good job, horse," Smith said. "Now you've done it."

The cowboys stood locked in their spots for a moment.

Smith grinned, said, "Howdy."

Slim went for his gun.

(4)

Smith drew swiftly and fired one of his silver bullets. The shot hit Slim solid in the chest and the power of the load knocked him on his bony ass.

Smith holstered the revolver and swung onto Shadow while the others were still trying to figure out how anyone could draw that fast. When they turned to respond, Smith and Shadow were already riding away in blast of night wind and racing shadows.

Slim stood up, put a finger in the hole in his chest. When he pulled it out, moonlight shined through. Slim wobbled a bit, said, "Ow dus id loog? Is id bag in duh bak?"

Zeke leaned around and looked at the Slim's back. There was a huge tear in the back of Slim's vest, and there were dry guts and bones and tendons sticking out of it.

"You're fine," Zeke said.

But in that moment Slim sizzled, then crumbled from the inside out. He fell apart into flaking pieces. The wind picked up the pieces and lifted them away as if they were nothing more than cigar ash.

"Goddamn it," Zeke said. "He done did in Slim. Must be shootin' silver."

Another of the cowboys said, "Come on, boys, let's get that son-of-a-bitch and eat him."

Smith was amazed at how fast Shadow could run and how smooth and comfortable he felt in the saddle. He was less comfortable looking over his shoulder and seeing the cowboys on their emaciated mounts riding hard in his direction, guns blazing.

He was certain of one thing however. Shadow could outrun them, and they needed some shooting lessons. Their shots weren't even coming near. But the thing that was in is head was: What in the hell is going on here, and who are those guys, or what are those guys, and what kind of shit has Snappy dropped me into?

And then Smith remembered his purpose. Wheeling Shadow, he started right back at them. It was wiser to run, but he had been sent on a mission by the Devil himself. He didn't entirely understand the mission, but he had to initiate action, get something going, see what it led to. He had been sent back because he was bold, not crafty, and he had only had three days to figure out how to put things back the way they were supposed to be.

Smith put the reins in his teeth, pulled both revolvers, clucked to Shadow, stuck him with the heels of his boots. The horse lunged forward, straight toward the cowboys, and when Shadow opened up, his body appeared longer and leaner, and the great strides he was taking brought him low to the ground.

(5)

They were like leaping shadows, Smith and his horse. They rode straight at the cowboys, and Smith fired both revolvers, and when he did, two of the cowboys jerked and went to ash right in the saddle. The horses, with their masters shot out of position, raced toward Smith.

As they neared, the moonlight caught in their teeth, and Smith could see those teeth were huge and shiny and sharp like daggers. It was, to say the least, a surprise.

Smith opened up with both guns on the horses, and when the silver bullets hit them, the charging mounts were reduced to scattering dust. Smith and Shadow rode right through the dust, into the midst of the cowboys. Bullets buzzed around Smith, but luck was with him. The only thing that got punctured was his saddle horn.

Smith popped off another of the cowboys, and then wheeled and rode out of the fray, bumping aside a horse with his own horse. A bullet snapped close to his ear; he could feel the wind from it all the way down to his ear drum.

The cowboys weren't able to turn on a dime like Shadow. They had to make big loops. One of them tried to wheel his horse, but the horse tripped and went down, throwing the cowboy. Smith shot the rider, destroying him. The horse regained its footing, came rushing at Smith, its teeth snapping, saliva flying in the moonlight. Another shot and that horse was dust too.

As Smith galloped away from the cowboys, feeling he had at least stirred the pot, though to what end he was uncertain, he saw a light in the distance. It was rocking back and forth, and it was growing as it came rapidly toward him.

The swinging light had shadow beneath it, and then it had shape, and the shape was a little wagon rig drawn by one small horse. The outfit was small, except for large wheels. There was a seat in the front, and a wagon bed in the back, small, compact, and stuffed with something. The light was from a lantern hanging on a post, sticking slightly out to the side of the rig. It swung back and forth as the rig neared.

Positioned on the seat was Undertaker, the man he had seen in the saloon a short time ago. No. A year ago by current time. The man was yelling and calling to the horse, slapping the reins, giving it all he could muster. And then, seemingly out of nowhere, Undertaker produced a torch, and without letting go of the reins, lit it quickly with a match, so quick, so smooth, Smith hardly saw it done.

For a moment, Smith thought the wagon rider was charging at him, but in a moment he realized Undertaker was going to pass him by, that he was heading straight for the cowboys with a vengeance. As the wagon passed, Smith saw that in the back of it were a number of bottles stuffed with rags. Smith had a pretty good idea what they were. Bottle bombs filled with kerosene. Undertaker now had the reins in his teeth, the torch in one hand, one of the rag-fused bottles clutched in the other.

One bounce too many, a bottle could break, the torch could drop, and Undertaker would go up in a light so brilliant one might think it was the rising of the morning sun. But he didn't go up. The next thing Smith knew, Undertaker was bearing down on one of the ghoul riders. The torch was touched to the fuse and the bottle was thrown. The ghoulish horse and rider burst into flames. The flames whipped over them like a fire in cotton shed. Man and horse were burned down to the ground so fast, all that was left were some sparks and a drift of black smoke that could be seen in the moonlight when it rose to the tree tops.

Smith rode Shadow back into the fray. Bullets zipped around his head. One punched lightly at his shirt, burned his shoulder, but darted on. Smith still had the reins of his mount in his teeth, and he had his Colts, and he was firing away. One of the nasties was riding straight for him. They were shortly less than twenty feet apart. The ghoul's pistol was drawn and he was surely about to fire as Smith's pistols clicked on empty. The next instant, the ghoul's head exploded like a gourd full of rotted seeds.

Smith glanced in the direction from which the shot had come, saw a gray horse with black withers and its rider coming quickly in his direction.

The rider was a woman. She was wearing a half mask that covered one side of her face. She was dressed in black from head to toe, a black hat with a red scarf tied around it. She had a coiled black snake whip draped over her shoulder, and a pair of revolvers were strapped to her waist. Her hair, even in the moonlight, appeared to be a flowing fire. She was holding a sawed-off shotgun, the stock of it sawed short as well. She had the but of it pressed against her thigh. She glanced at Smith, reined her horse to a stop, jerked the shotgun open, popping out the two dispensed shells. She flipped the reins over her lap and the horse stopped short. She fished two shotgun shells out of her pocket and filled the barrels, snapped the weapon shut with a flick of her wrist, took hold of her reins with her free hand.

Smith knew immediately it was Payday.

She rode up beside him. Smith realized she didn't recognize him now that he looked younger and was minus his mustache. She said, "You ought to quit looking at me, and finish what you started here."

"You're a lot to look at."

She turned the masked side of her face away from him, self-consciously. He realized she had misunderstood his meaning. Smith turned his head in time to see Undertaker whipping his wagon around, tossing bottles, smashing them into more of the cowpokes. Cowpokes and horses burst into flames, immediately became a smoldering mess of wind-whipped dust blowing close to the ground.

"Shall we finish?" Payday said.

"Not sure we're needed," Smith said, nodding at Undertaker.

"Maybe not," Payday said. "But there's still a few of them, and what fun is it watching someone else do all the work?"

Payday used her free hand to pull the whip off her shoulder as she slipped the shotgun into a sheath on the saddle at the same time with the other. She put her heels to her mount and sprang forward, straight into what remained of the fray.

As she did, one of the horses, minus its rider, came directly at Smith and Shadow.

Shadow reared and slashed out with its hooves. The ghoul horse snapped its teeth in the air, tried to bite. Shadow was too quick. Its hooves caught the horse in the head and knocked it down. The horse turned to powder. It was then that Smith realized the Shadow's horseshoes were made of pure silver.

(6)

One of the cowpokes decided escape was the better part of valor, but by the time he turned his horse, Payday was standing up in the stirrups, snapping the whip, catching the cowboy around the bicep. The whip wrapped like a constrictor, tightened. With a wrenching motion of the whip, the ghoul's near-desiccated arm snapped off and flew into the air, and fell to the ground. The cowboy turned, used his good hand to grab his pistol and fire. It was a bad miss. He might as well have been throwing a rock at a gnat's ass at a thousand yards.

Payday rode past him and wheeled in the saddle, swinging her legs around smoothly until she was facing backwards, and the whip cracked again. This time it caught the cowpoke's neck, and with a yank, she jerked the dead rider's head off. His horse rode away with the headless cowboy still working the reins, putting heels to his ghoulish steed. Payday swung around to the front of the saddle, put her heels to her own mount, closed the gap, cracked the whip, snatched him off his horse and busted him on the ground so hard pieces of him came off. The headless ghoul got up, stumbled around, and then collapsed into a pile of rotting meat.

Nearby, another ghoul had taken one of Undertaker's bottles in the teeth and had gone up in a gust of flame and burst of smoke.

Smith and Shadow stopped and were watching as Smith casually reloaded his weapons with his silver bullets. It was quite a show. Smith pulled a boot from the stirrup and slung his leg over his saddle and sat relaxed.

"They've had some practice at this," Smith said to Shadow.

The remaining two cowboys broke for it, riding out to Smith's left as fast as they could go, Payday, and Undertaker in his little wagon, were in hot pursuit. Smith casually lifted one of his revolvers and fired, striking one the riders in the head with a silver bullet, knocking him off his horse, causing him to puff into a billion tiny particles. The horse escaped, and the last rider and his mount had a good lead and were soon gone. Payday and Undertaker turned around and headed in Smith's direction.

Payday came up on Smith's left side, Undertaker the right.

"Ain't never seen them explode like that from anything but fire," Undertaker said. "Shotgun blast will do it if it messes them up just right, ripping them to pieces will do it, and fire will do it, but I ain't never seen bullets kill them."

"Silver bullets," Smith said.

"Silver?" Undertaker said. "That works?"

"You seen it."

Payday said, "Silver or not, we best get to a safe place. There's still a bunch of them roaming around out here, and the one that got away is sure to bring trouble."

"You don't seem to mind trouble," Smith said, and smiled at Payday.

"Yeah, but I get tired of it from time to time."

They traveled for awhile along a forest trail. It was quiet and cool and beautiful. As Smith rode beside Payday, he said, "I'd pay to see you work, lady."

"Many have, in a manner of speaking," she said. "Any other time, you'd have to."

Undertaker's wagon rattled up on the opposite side of Smith. "Well, just the one horse and one rider got away," he said.

"Gives us something to kill later," Payday said.

"That's all that's left?" Smith said.

Payday turned her head so she could focus on Smith with her good eye. "Hell no. There's plenty of them to go around. So keep your pistol loaded."

"Always do," Smith said.

"I saw that they eat...people."

"They do," Payday said. "They do indeed."

A waterfall shimmered in the moonlight, cascaded thunderously down the mountainside and smashed into the rocks below and joined the fast moving stream that twisted along amongst the tall trees. They rode into the stream, wagon and horses, and avoiding the rocks, took a smooth path in the water bed, directly into the falls. The falling water put the lantern on the wagon out with a hiss.

Under the falls was an enormous cave. Moonlight snuck through the lines of water and gave the interior a soft, silver glow. All manner of odds and ends were strewn about. It was as if a General Store and a barn had exploded. Rope, saddles, barrels, crates. A couple of horses standing at ready. A pile of hay. A crude wheelchair. The cave smelled of water and wet soil and hay and horse manure. Smith noted that the walls crawled with veins of silver.

Payday and Smith dismounted as Undertaker pulled up beside the wheelchair. As he worked his way out of the wagon and into the chair, Smith saw both legs were gone below the knee. All of him had been there last time he had seen him in the saloon. Whatever was going on here a year later wasn't a carnival. Like Snappy had said, there had been some changes.

Undertaker wheeled the chair with one hand, took hold of the reins of his horse with the other, and led it to the pile of hay to eat. Payday followed suit. Smith led Shadow over.

Entering from a smaller tunnel, walking, looking somewhat more ragged than before, was Doc. He eyed Smith, and then looked at Payday.

"He's all right," she said. "He killed some ghouls."

Undertaker dropped the reins of his horse by the hay, wheeled himself around and closer to Payday. He reached inside his jacket and pulled out a small black book and a stubby pencil. He wet the end of the pencil with his tongue. He said, "How many ghouls did we get tonight?"

"I don't know exactly," Payday said. "Counting what our friend here got, seven or eight, more or less. I'm not sure."

"Closer to eleven or twelve," Smith said. "Those fire bombs did some business."

Undertaker cocked his head, thinking, then turned and wrote in his book. "Not exact count, but that makes about two hundred or so down."

"So what's left?" Doc said.

"Ought to be close to a hundred or more. Possibly two hundred, as there's some we ain't figured. But there's no more than that."

"No more than what?" Smith said. "Close to a hundred. Maybe two hundred. Perhaps more. That isn't exactly fine arithmetic at work."

"Yeah, I know. We really got no idea. I just like to keep count of the dead ones. Doc always asks what's left, and I always pretend I know. Makes me feel like we're getting somewhere. Truth is, they never seem to end."

"And the horses change too," Smith said.

Undertaker nodded. "Yep. You saw it. Don't have no effect on other animals, just men and horses. They are hungry and willing to do whatever their master asks of them."

"Who would that be?" Smith said, knowing full well the answer.

"Quill," Payday said.

"And what do they eat when there's nothing to eat?" Smith asked.

"I don't think they're eating much these days," Doc said. "They done ate most everybody up. But them being hungry as they are, that's what makes them even more dangerous. They don't die of it, not eating, but they stay famished and ready to eat, and if they get hold of one of us, they'll rip us apart faster than a chicken at Sunday dinner. And who did you say you were?"

"I didn't. Smith will do."

"He shoots silver, Doc," Undertaker said. "It hits them, they turn to dust. Don't have to have their bodies blasted or ripped apart. Beats anything I've ever seen."

"These days I see something that beats anything I've ever seen on a daily basis," Doc said.

"The dead don't bother you here, do they," Smith said.

"Don't know we're here," Doc said. He eyeballed Smith. "Way we work is we pick our fights. We go out at night, which is when they like to prowl. They can move around in the day, but they're lethargic, like sick possums.

Rest of the time, we hide out in this cave. So far they haven't found us. Last night, I wasn't part of it. Not up to snuff. But I'm fine now."

"Seems when they're poorly would be the best time," Smith said.

"They hole up mostly then," Doc said. "They can come out if they want, but they're more active at night, and we're more likely to find them and kill them."

Smith nodded, looked around the cave. "Do much mining?"

"What?" Doc said.

"See those veins in the wall of your cave? Even if they found you, they wouldn't...couldn't come in here. That's silver. It doesn't have to be in a bullet. From what I understand, they don't even like being around it."

"I thought it was just some kind of pretty rock," Doc said.

"In a way, that's exactly what it is," Smith said.

Undertaker laughed. "That's something. All the silver found around these parts, and it never occurred to me they don't like it. When they were alive, lots of them mined for it, or tried to take it at the card table, but now they don't want any of it. That's pretty damn funny."

"Are you folks all that's left?" Smith asked.

"Don't know for sure," Payday said.

"We saw some live ones not too long ago," Undertaker said. "They were being chased by ghouls. We wanted to help them, but there was too much distance and too many ghouls. We hope they outran them. They had good horses, so maybe."

"Most likely some Indians are somewhere in the hills," Doc said. "They don't want to be seen, good chance you ain't gonna be seen, by the living or the dead."

Payday had grown quiet. Smith watched as she watched him carefully. She said, "I knew a Smith once. I didn't like him."

"Where you from?" Doc asked.

"Way down South."

Payday eyed Smith. "How'd you know about the silver? That it would do what it does to those ghouls?"

"Lucky guess, I suppose," Smith said.

"You just happen to have a gun with silver bullets in it?" she said. "A horse with silver shoes?"

"Don't look a gift horse in the mouth," Undertaker said.

Payday said, "You remind me of someone."

"I was just thinking the same thing about you," Smith said.

Payday, without thinking, touched a hand to her eye patch. "You can bet you don't know me," she said.

Undertaker said, "I was thinking I'd seen you too, Smith. Just don't know where."

"Not likely," Smith said, and walked over to Shadow and removed his saddle. He tossed it on the ground. "Don't know about the rest of you, but soon as I get my horse taken care of, I'm gonna stretch out and rest. I need it."

⟨8⟩

The morning sun rose up and so did the cave's occupants. When Smith pulled his boots on, he smelled meat cooking. Across the way he saw that Payday had a fire going and was frying bacon in a huge, black skillet. A pot of coffee was on the fire as well. The cooking bacon and boiling coffee smelled great.

Near the front of the cave, Undertaker was wrapping his amputated legs in fresh white dressings, and Doc was sipping a sarsaparilla to hold off the whisky urge. Smith knew right off he was a drunk that was trying to quit. He had seen him drunk in the salon. He knew about drunks. His father had been one.

Smith rolled up his blanket, put it on his saddle, wandered over to Payday. She wasn't wearing her hat. Her long, red hair fell like a bloody waterfall to her shoulders. She had on her eye patch, and when she saw Smith, he noticed that she moved so that the "good" side of her face was toward him.

"You want some bacon?" Payday asked.

"Sure. Thanks."

Undertaker had positioned himself in his wheelchair, and he rolled up next to Smith. Smith looked at him, then his fresh-wrapped legs, said, "What happened?"

"You get straight to somethin', don't you?" Undertaker asked.

"I guess so."

"He didn't ask me about my eye patch," Payday said.

"You don't want to talk about it, you don't have to," Smith said, looking at Undertaker.

"Hell, it's okay," Undertaker said. "I'll talk about it. I'm just wondering where you came from. You said way down South, but you don't mean lately do you? What I don't get is how you got in here. You ain't from the town. I can tell that. But you just showed up. How? We've tried riding out. You can't. There's some kind of invisible wall that keeps you from it."

"You can ride in," Smith said, "it's just you can't ride out. I figure whatever is making all this happen likes the idea of new folks coming in, but not leaving. I would be one of the new folks."

"Food for the ghouls," Payday said.

Smith nodded.

Doc walked up, said, "Undertaker gets sidetracked easy. He was gonna tell you how he lost his legs."

Undertaker said, "Oh, yeah. I did start that story, didn't I?"

"Actually," Doc said, "you almost started it. You want me or Payday to tell it for you. We might even make it a better story."

"No," Undertaker said, "I'll tell it." Undertaker positioned his wheelchair so that he could get a good look at Smith, and started. "Year or so back, fella named Trumbo Quill changed."

"That's one way of putting it," Payday said.

"He was bad enough before, but suddenly he ain't really Quill. He's some kind of lizard and bird mix in pants. In the beginning he didn't wear pants. I don't think modestly caused him to start wearing them. I think he kept snagging his well rope on things, so he got him some pants. He's an ugly bastard, I'll tell you that."

"About the legs," Doc said.

"Leading up to it," Undertaker said. "One's got to do with the other, don't it? So, this Quill, he went really wicked. You wouldn't think he could jump into that wicked business any deeper than he was, 'cause he was already one mean son-of-a-bitch, but he could. And he did. It was like something crawled up his ass and sprouted inside him. He had this thing happen to him one night in the saloon, top floor, up there with a gal. And down he comes, all winged and ugly and meaner a snake. Snatches the head off the gal, tears folks up. I managed to get out of there without getting hurt. Doc and Payday weren't there, so they were all right."

"I was in Doc's office," Payday said. "Recovering from what Quill had done to my eye. Before he changed. He cut it out, Smith. Right out… There was a man in the saloon the night it happened. His name was Smith. That's the Smith I know that I don't like."

"There's a lot of Smiths," Smith said.

"Oh, it wasn't you. But, I got to tell you, you remind me of him. That's who it is you remind me of. The other Smith."

"Yep," Undertaker said. "Me too. But you're younger, face is different, but there's a familiarity about the two of you. You could easily be cousins."

"You were saying about Quill," Smith said.

"Well," Undertaker said, "Quill went to work on the town, killing and maiming. I hid out near the cemetery, and danged if that wasn't where he went. Flying. Now you can believe me or not, but he has wings and he can fly like a goddamn bird."

"I believe you," Smith said.

"You do?"

"After what I seen last night, why not?"

"You're sure dealing with all this mighty well, mister," Payday said.

"My people were a calm lot," Smith said. "I inherited the same traits."

"Your whole family use silver bullets?" Payday asked.

"Absolutely," Smith said.

"Kind of expensive, ain't it?"

"Pretty much," Smith said. "Why I'm a good shot. Less expensive when you don't miss. All right now, Quill was flying."

"He flew over the cemetery, muttering words that made my skin grow cold, made the pit of my stomach turn to ice. I can't explain it any better than that. The words themselves was like weapons. All I could do was stay hid in a clutch of trees out near Boot Hill. And then, here's what happened, son. Them dead folks started coming out of the ground. It was them words Quill was muttering. He was bringing them back to life. Or life of a sorts. They clawed and kicked and bit their way out of them graves. They all stood up and faced Quill, who had come to rest on a tombstone like a roosting chicken. He said something to them, and then he took to the sky, and them dead folks, they started following, walking under his shadow as he flew toward town."

"And that was just the beginning," Doc said.

"Yeah, I should have lit out right then," Undertaker said, "but I didn't. I followed behind the buildings, and moved down an alley, and got to where I could see them. Quill landed and went into the saloon, just the way he always had. Some of the dead went in there too. Some went down the street and broke into places and took themselves some guns and such. And then, down at the bone yard, out back of the town, where they drag off all the dead horses, them that still had some flesh and brains, stood up. Their horse faces got twisted and long snouted, just like the folks from Boot Hill got twisted up and long faced. You seen how they looked last night. Some are more rotten than others, some in passable shape.

"Anyway, the horses changed up and went ugly, came down the street and waited there until them ghouls found them a mount and saddled up. I seen all this hiding out by the garbage cans in that alley. I found a way into the General store through a window wasn't good shut, and hid up in the attic where the coffee and such was stored. There's a little window up there, and I used it to spy. During the day, when they were sleeping, or less active, I'd sneak down and steal me a can of peaches. I stole a knife, and I used that to open up food cans. I slept behind bags of coffee and corn meal. I shared some of that raw corn meal with a rat. Me and him kind of became pals. I chewed some of the coffee beans. Later on, feeling more hungry than friendly, I killed and ate the rat. I ain't proud of it, but I ate him raw. Not tasty, sir. Not tasty. And a betrayal to our friendship."

"So, I'm hid up in that loft, and as the days went on them dead folks was fishing towns people out here and there, eatin' em, and not with taters. Some they was just biting, so they'd turn. I don't know how they choose to do what to, but that's how it was. I was down in the General Store one mornin', tryin' to find some canned goods to take up to the loft. I was thinking of bagging up some, and when it got high day, I was gonna light out for the woods and the mountains. While I was down there I found me a good revolver and a rifle too, some ammo. But before I could tote it up to my nest, I looked up, and there at the outside window, a face was pressed against the glass, staring at me. It was one of them damn ghouls. It was broad daylight, but this one was out and about. To make a long story short—"

"Ha!" Doc said.

Undertaker gave him a hard look, and continued. "As I was saying, before I was so rudely interrupted, to make a long story short, that ghoul sounded the alarm. I tried to go out into the back alley, but they were coming down it, right at me. Turning back, I found they were now coming out of the back door of the General Store. I was trapped like a roach in a gun barrel. I didn't have that gun I had taken from the store loaded, so I dropped it and the food, made for this open window I seen in the alley wall. I dove through. Mostly. My legs didn't make it. The eaters got hold of me and went to chewing. I was being eaten alive. That's when hands pulled me on through. Doc and Payday here. They had been hiding in that building, which was the bank, hiding there the same as I had been hiding at the store.

"Doc and Payday hauled me out of there and on out to the horses they had in a lot near a side door of the bank. They had been within minutes of leaving anyway, having gathered a bunch of supplies and having found those horses. Funny thing was, they had been hiding in the bank, slipping in and out of that window, getting food for themselves from the same General store. Our paths had never crossed. I hadn't even noticed any food was missing. I guess I thought it was me eating it all. Payday and Doc put me on the back of Payday's horse, and we stormed out of there before them ghouls could finish picking my pants and legs out of their teeth. You see, them ghouls are a little on the slow side during the day, and not too bright any time. It was a clean getaway, except I didn't take my legs with me.

"Doc knew about this old cave up here, so this is where we ended up. He and Payday worked on my legs, sawed off the useless bone and cauterized the wounds, did what could be done. Cut them off well above the bites, so I didn't end up changing like the others. Hadn't been for them, I'd have been a goner for sure. Would have turned ghoulish. Way I look at it, me and Payday and Doc are kin now."

"We were just in the right place at the right time," Doc said. "Don't make more of it than you ought to."

Undertaker kept on with his story.

"We been going back into town and parts hereabout now and again, trying to kill as many of them dead things as we can, stealing supplies. Quill, he's the key, but he's too powerful, and we don't know where he's holed up. We gathered up a few more escapees from the town to help us. Guess there must have been a dozen of us once. But in time we were whittled down to what you see now. Quill got most of them, the ghouls got the rest. Like I said, the real source of our problem is Quill."

"I'll help you kill him," Smith said.

"Glad to have you," Doc said. "But I want to warn you, I don't know even silver bullets can kill Quill. I mean, hell, you make it sound easy. Just waltz in there and kill Quill, and back to the house. You got to get through the ghouls first, and the town, that's their sanctuary. Quill, he's usually at the saloon, but he's got some other hiding place we ain't figured, and he's a beast, a monster. It's not like he's an angry guy with a pistol. We did mention he could fly and had magic words and stuff, right?"

"I figure from what you've said, mid-day is the best time to kill them," Smith said.

"I'll say one thing for you," Doc said. "You're focused. You did hear all that I said about magic words, a flying ugly critter, dead riders and such. Just because you survived a bunch of dead cowboys, doesn't mean you can outshoot and outfight a town full of them. And then, if you did, you still got the flying boy to mess with. And he is quite temperamental. During the day they may be slow, but they're also hid."

"Noted," Smith said. "You've got more experience with these ghouls than I do, but I got my talents. Once Quill's dead, I can ride out of this patch of country and the bad stuff is over. He's the key. Best to face a problem head on, and I'm best by myself."

"You won't be alone," Payday said. "There'll be plenty of ghouls to keep you company."

"Oh bullshit," Undertaker said. "We ain't letting you ride in by yourself. We've killed more ghouls than you've even seen. You need us. Besides, you can't keep us from coming if we want to."

"I'm not asking that of you," Smith said.

"Like he said," Doc said. "We do it all the time, so you aren't really asking anything special of us. But before we start riding and shooting, let's eat some of that bacon."

(9)

As they rode out, Undertaker in his wagon full of explosives, everyone else mounted on a horse, Doc with a shotgun, Payday with her sawed-off and whip, Smith thought: Here we go, a band of cripples. One missing legs, another an eye, a drunk, and one brought back from the dead. All we need now is a headless dog to drag around.

Thing they don't know that I know, Smith thought, and I don't have any urge to tell them, just yet, is our time is short. Three days, Snappy said. Three days. And on top of that, I'm supposed to beware a long dark night and two moons.

Smith was considering all of this when they came to a tree-covered rise of land just outside of town. They paused and looked down.

Doc said, "They sleep during the day. They can move, but they're like bats. They don't like the light. But the thing is, slow, or not, there's still a lot of them and they can eat your ass if they get hold of you."

"You keep saying that," Smith said.

"When there were more of us, we'd raid the town during the day, kill them off. But they started rigging the place with booby traps. And that's how we got whittled down."

"That's something you didn't mention before," Smith said.

"We decided Indian tactics were best for fighting an overwhelming force. Least until today. Today, we decided to do something stupid."

"You can go back you want," Smith said. "I've made it clear I'm not asking anyone for anything."

"You wouldn't, would you?" Payday said.

"What's that mean?" Smith said.

"It means you're an idiot. You go down there by yourself, you won't come back."

Smith turned in the saddle and looked at her. He decided maybe he did need to tell them, though believing him was another matter. He said, "What if I told you I knew there was a time schedule. Three days. At the end of those three days, Quill will be so powerful, nothing will stop him. Silver, dropping a mountain on him. Nothing… And don't ask how I know. I know. So, I don't have time to fool around, savvy?"

"What makes you so special?" Payday said.

"Payday," Doc said. "Forget it. He knew about the silver, and he killed ghouls, and I got a feeling he knows what we need to know, and I said it before, and I'll say it again. I don't care how he knows it, or who he is, or where he came from. I'm with him, even if I do think this is a dumb idea."

Undertaker raised a hand. "Count me in."

Smith looked at Payday. Payday gave Smith a look that could boil water. "Same," she said.

"Now, I'm not the idiot Payday thinks I am," Smith said. "We're going in, but we're still gonna be sneaky as mice in a pantry. We're gonna see if we can find Quill and kill him, and if we don't, we're gonna do as much damage to their operation as possible."

"That means were gonna kill and burn stuff, right?" Undertaker said.

"Something like that."

"Good. A nice fire in the morning gets me stimulated."

"I still think you're an idiot," Payday said.

They dismounted and moved closer to town by leading their horses. Except Undertaker, of course. He rode in his wagon. They made their way to town through a dry draw that would eventually lead behind the buildings, near the General Store. If they were careful, the draw was deep enough they could get close without being seen. It was also an obvious place for a trap, and when they came to a dark patch of ground, Smith said, "Hold it a moment."

Smith bent down and looked. The ground in the draw was dark there, covered in pine needles, but on either side of it, the needles were sparse. Smith bent down and picked at the edge of the pile, found it was all connected by thin limbs and vines. Underneath was a large pit with spikes in it.

"Crude," Smith said.

"Had we come by night, like we have before, down this draw, it would have got us," Undertaker said.

"They may be getting smarter," Doc said. "They know this draw is a blind spot, so, they trapped it. Can't tell you how many times we've used this path to get into town."

They took the chance of leading their horses out of the draw, and around the trap. They didn't go back in the draw, safe as it was with them not being in eye line. They came to the edge of the town and stopped within a cluster of trees not far from the General store and the livery.

"The livery is the closest," Doc said. "I suggest we start there."

They left the horses in the stand of trees, except for Undertaker, who had his little horse pull his wagon into town slightly ahead of the others. He lit a torch as they went, stuck it in a metal stand on the side of the wagon. The torch was covered in pitch, and it burned steadily.

The streets were empty and it was quiet as the grave, which seemed appropriate. They stopped in front of the livery, paused at the huge double doors.

"I'd be a mite careful going in," Doc said.

"Everyone move to the side," Smith said. "Doc, except you. You take one door, I'll take another. But be quick to move."

They jerked the doors open and jumped back. A huge log with a number of knives on one end, swung down from the rafters, through the doorway, and back with a thudding sound. It swung back and forth for a few moments, then stopped.

"That could have been messy," Payday said.

"Means they're here," Smith said.

Smith dropped to one knee and looked at the ground that led into the livery. There was a tarp there covered in a thin layer of dirt. "Another pit, right here in front of the door. Probably another at the rear. It's not very wide, but my guess is it's got some nasty things waiting below. Sharp objects probably."

Smith studied the ground, decided he could see where it was solid.

He backed off, prepared to jump.

Payday said, "You're sure."

"You made me hesitate," he said.

"Maybe you should hesitate," she said.

"Just stay ready, all of you."

Smith backed off and jumped over the narrow pit. Once inside the livery he paused to let his eyes adjust to the dark. He found a couple of wide planks and wrestled them over the pit; he assumed this was what they were for.

Undertaker rode over the planks with his horse pulling him in his little wagon. His torch gave the place a bit of light, and in the light they could see them. Cowboy ghouls, hanging upside down by their boots and spurs in the rafters, holding their hats to their chests with crossed arms. Their revolvers weren't in their holsters, but were jammed tight in their belts. Smith and his companions looked at the situation in awe, the dead ghouls hanging there like rotten fruit, at least a dozen of them. Noises hadn't bothered them, but the torch light did. Their eyes popped open and glowed red and they kicked loose of the rafters and fell, twisting like cats to land on their feet, planting their hats on their heads in one fluid motion. They drew their guns from their belts, fired, but their shots were way off, their eyes squinted against the sunlight coming in through the door.

Smith drew his pistols and Undertaker lit a rag sticking out of a bottle and tossed it. His horse, trained for such a thing, didn't even startle when the explosive went off and wiped out three ghouls in a sweep of flame that sent them running wildly into the hay, setting it afire.

Smith fired his pistols. He moved quickly, twisting left and right, going down on one knee to avoid the ghouls' wild shooting, then he came up again, still firing. Four ghouls vibrated and turned to dust.

Payday and Doc opened up with shotguns. They hit ghouls, but not solidly enough. A before unseen ghoul dropped down on Payday's shoulders. She bent forward and the ghoul flipped over her head. Her shotgun was empty, so when the ghoul came to its feet, wheeled at her with a sound like a hissing cat, she hit it in the face with the sawed-off stock, kicked out and caught it in the stomach, knocked it back. She dropped the shotgun and pulled the whip off her shoulder. She stepped wide left and let the whip flash out. It plucked an eye from the ghoul as easily as picking a grape from a vine. Another snap, another eye. The ghoul wandered blind. Doc, stepped forward, his double barrel reloaded, fired, and cut the ghoul's head off its shoulders.

Now Undertaker had a lit bottle in either hand, and he tossed them, the bottles exploding in the back of the livery. Ghouls jumped out of hiding from mildewed hay piles and from behind stacks of old saddles. There were a lot of them, waking up late to the action. They were on fire. The flaming monsters ran about like crazed rats.

Now ghouls dropped down from the hay loft like pigeon shit. One, soon as it landed on the ground, pulled its pistol and fired. The shot grazed Payday's side. She had recovered her shotgun and had it loaded now, and she cut down with one barrel, taking her attacker him off at the knees. The other barrel took its head.

Carefully they backed as the ghouls came, over the boards, over the pit. Once they were out in the open, Smith kicked the boards loose. They fell onto the dirt covered canvas and collapsed it. Wooden spikes poked up through the canvas. One of the burning ghouls, wandering blindly about, tumbled into the pit and was pin-cushioned by the spikes, setting the tarp on fire.

"Now's the time to light 'em up good," Undertaker said.

Smith and the others grabbed at Undertaker's bottles, lit them off his torch, and tossed them inside the livery. Flames raced throughout, climbed stairs, wagged fire tongues from one end of the livery to the other. Bodies moved inside the flames and collapsed in exploding dust heaps. Boards creaked and blackened. Fire wiggled through slits in the rafters, the livery sagged. More ghouls tumbled into the pit.

The back door of the barn was knocked off its hinges by a mass of desperate ghouls. One of their contraptions, forgotten in their panic, another log with knives, swung down and pinned a half dozen of them as they charged out of the back door. The place was swiftly an inferno.

"That should get Quill's attention," Undertaker said.

They gathered their horses in the trees and rode them boldly up Main Street. Most of the stores had been ransacked. Doors banged open, windows knocked out. They came to the Falling Rock Mining Assay Office and found it surprisingly in order, continued, checking stores. Not a sign of a soul, or a soulless, anywhere. They came to the bell tower adjacent to the church. Payday shoved open the door and jumped inside, the shotgun at the ready. Smith plowed in after her while the others watched outside. No one was there.

Payday and Smith moved beneath the bell and looked up. Nothing but the bell and the dangling rope were visible, the gaps on all four sides of the bell that allowed it to swing out and back, and for its sound to bang about throughout the town.

"This place makes my skin crawl," Payday said.

"Bells bother you?"

"Of course not. Can't you feel it?"

"I feel that way just about anywhere in this town."

"Let's go," Payday said.

As they headed toward the door, Smith said, "That was dumb. Jumping in like that. There could have been a hundred of them."

"There were plenty in the livery barn, and you were right there with me and the others. When you do something stupid, it's brave, and when I do it's dumb."

"It was dumb when I did it," Smith said. "But we killed a mass of them."

"It's only a matter of minutes before the rest of them start coming out of their holes. Far more than were in the barn. Keep that in mind. We have made a dent, and it's my opinion, we should now light a shuck and head out."

"Noted."

As they rode down the street, out of town, they paused at the General Store. Smith said, "I saw two barrels of kerosene out front, rolled out on the ground. Undertaker, you pull your wagon over, me and Doc will load them."

"Who died and made you king?" Payday asked.

Smith sighed. "I saw two barrels of kerosene. I thought it would give Undertaker more fuel for his bottles. We can also take bottles from inside, use the goods in them, then have Undertaker fill them up with kerosene. But, now you know the material is here, what would you do?"

It was Payday's turn to sigh. "I'd load the barrels and get what food we can find," she said.

"That's a hell of an idea," Smith said. "Wish I'd thought of it."

"Yeah," Doc said, "that's an alright idea unless Quill comes along."

"Then we better load up and go," Undertaker said. "I thought I had the last of the kerosene, but those dumb fools probably pushed it out here out of the way so they could chase the rats inside and eat them. Let's hurry."

(10)

The sun went down and the dead came out from their hiding places in town buildings and from the graveyard where many scrambled to as night ended, pulling dirt and leaves in after them, able to walk in daylight, but not happy about it. Some lay in the woods under big trees with wide boughs, lay where the shadows were thick. Their horses lay with them, or were lying until needed in barns outside of town, in houses, and even in town in stores and businesses.

Out in the forest, some of the ghouls hung upside down from limbs, or lay stretched across limbs like lizards, hats pulled down tight. They lay anywhere the shadow was deep, letting their dead selves recharge, and then when night came, they rose up in hunger and in need of old patterns; rose up and walked or rode their dead horses out of the forest and out of the barns and out of the stores along main street, out from wherever they hid.

Their main destination was, as in life, the saloon.

That night the Sundown Saloon was lit up with lantern light and it was full of ghouls. Cowboys and dead saloon girls. Laughing and dancing to the sound of the piano, which sounded as if it were missing a few keys because it was. The night before one of the ghouls, to prove his marksmanship, had delivered a few notes via .44 slugs, knocking off a few ivories. He had been aiming at a glass on top of the piano. The glass was still there.

Against the bar two ghouls leaned their backs, staring out at the dancers, nursing beers. When they drank, the beer oozed out of the rotten rips in their bodies. Flies decorated their mouths while they talked. "Got to tell you, Gene," the one named Roy said, causing a disruption of flies from around his mouth, "all these damn boot hill women are so ugly they'd have to sneak up on a bottle of whisky and shoot it to get a drink."

"That's a fact, except for the one over there by the piano, she looks pretty good, though her ass fell off last night."

"Say it did?"

Gene nodded. "It's still over there by the piano."

"Later, no one's looking we can pick it up," Roy said.

"Well, that's something to consider on. How do you think she keeps her balance, her ass gone and all?"

Roy studied on that for a moment, dug a toothpick out of his shirt pocket and poked it around between his four teeth. "It's the feet. She's got big feet. You got feet big enough, you can stack an elephant on them and they won't fall over. Course, it helps there's legs on top of the feet. Kind of works like a two legged table that way, but it's the support matters. It's the feet."

"You, my friend, are a goddamn scientist and philosopher."

"I know it," Roy said. "But I try to be modest."

They leaned and considered for awhile. Then Gene said, "Bad about the barn, wasn't it?"

"Yeah, bites the dog's ass to have been them," Roy said.

"You won't catch me sleeping in the barn. I got me a good place."

"I guess so, we got the same damn place, fool."

"That's right, buddy, and we're ahead of the curve when it comes to being safe."

"Course," Roy said, "those horrible bastards are always shooting and killing somebody. Why don't they just let us kill 'em and get it over with? That's what I want to know. Ain't like they're gonna come out on top."

"They're stubborn," Gene said.

"It's the way the living are, and I'll say what you're thinking, what we're all thinking, we don't need their kind around here."

"They are good to eat."

Roy smacked his lips. "Well, all right. They got that going for them, but I'd rather eat rats. Hard to catch, but they don't shoot back."

"That's a point you got there, Roy."

"Oh, shit, here comes Quill. And he looks pissed."

"He always looks pissed."

Quill came in through into the saloon, flexing his leather wings. He was bigger than before and had taken on a mummified look, as if he had been wet down good and dried in the sun. Had more teeth than before, more teeth every time they saw him, more teeth than a mouth should hold; they poked in all directions. The piano stopped playing, and except for a long, slow fart easing out of a ghoul's foul digestion, the saloon was as silent as the face of the moon.

Chairs clattered, bottles rolled off tables and crashed to the floor. The ghouls were hustling as if a fire were at the door. A couple of ghouls slipped out the back. Quill looked at the rest of them. He moved amongst the tables, looking left and right. Finally, he chose one of the ghouls, grabbed him by the neck and squeezed until the man's head flew off in a spray of blood. He dropped the truly dead body of the ghoul, and looked about the saloon. His wings flexed silently and his long tail quivered.

"You just let them ride into town and kill a bunch of you," Quill said, snapping the blood off his fingers. "That ain't good business. That ain't good nothin'. It don't happen no more, you hear. Let me show you why."

Quill moved like a shot, grabbed one of the men's arms and jerked it off with a ripping of bone and shirt cloth, and swung it into the teeth of another ghoul, knocking him over a table.

"Cause it does, they won't have to kill you. I will." Quill handed the ghoul back his arm. "Souvenir," he said. "Any questions?"

"If I sew this on, will it grow back?" said the ghoul holding his arm.

Quill slammed his fist down so hard on the ghoul's head, the skull fragmented like a rock dropped on a pumpkin.

"Now," Quill said. "Any more questions?"

There were none.

PART FOUR:
Quill Hunting

Come out, come out, wherever you are.
FROM THE CHILDREN'S GAME OF HIDE AND SEEK

(1)

Come daybreak, Smith was saddling up Shadow. Undertaker, Doc, and Payday were watching.

"What are you doing?" Payday asked.

"I'm building a chicken coop," he said.

"Smart ass," she said.

"Taking another run," Smith said. "We did good yesterday, but all we did was kill ghouls. Now there are two days left, and I have to stop Quill, and what's about to happen. And I have no idea how to do it."

Undertaker rolled his chair over. "We keep saying, cut them down one at a time, and eventually he won't have any helpers."

"You don't believe me about the time limit, that's the thing," Smith said.

"It's more we don't understand about the time limit."

Smith finished tightening a cinch strap. "Get Quill, you're through. He's the source of it all. He runs the show. Here's as much as I know, and all I can tell you is I know."

"That's what preachers say," Doc said. "It's easy to sell the invisible. Cheap overhead."

Smith turned to look at them, his back against Shadow.

"In two days time, Quill will become so powerful, that he will open a gate of some sort…I don't know exactly. And some nasty son-of-a-bitches called The Old Ones are going to come through it, and that's all she wrote. Nothing to do then to stop them, and Quill will become a big dog. Maybe one of them. Maybe their ruler. Hell, he might be their lieutenant or their janitor. It doesn't make any difference. All of us will be done for, and it won't just be death. I've seen some things worse than death, and according to a very good source, this is even worse, because there's no merit system involved. Hellfire and damnation compared to The Old Ones is like comparing a stick horse to the real thing. I thought yesterday I'd stir Quill out of hiding. We didn't. I think he thought his army of rot would take care of us, so why bother. He may feel different now. He may want to come out and do the deed himself. This time, I'm going to raise some real hell, wake the bastard up."

"Still, we just have your word about the two days," Payday said.

"That's right," Smith said. "That's all you got."

"Yesterday we were lucky," Payday said. "That's all."

"Way you do it, is you get you prey in your sights, and you just keep coming," Smith said. "They run, you push after them. They hide, you dig them out. I learned that from experience."

"You were a bounty hunter?" Doc asked.

"That and lots of other things."

"We can't go with you again," Doc said. "One time in was all right. I thought I was being stupid then, and now I figure I was right. Like Payday said, we were just lucky."

"I said we had two days," Smith said. "I wasn't exaggerating. I don't care if you believe me or not. I'm tired of repeating myself."

Smith mounted up.

"They'll be expecting you," Doc said.

"Noted," Smith said.

"If you got to go, my guess is he's in the saloon," Undertaker said. "He ain't always there, but he's there plenty. That's where I'd start. We don't go there because we know he's there a lot. We never thought a straight-on conflict with him was a good idea. You know, that whole whittling theory of ours."

"Thanks," Smith said.

"You're a fool and a blockhead," Payday said.

"Also true," Smith said, tipping his hat. He clucked to Shadow and they rode off, through the waterfall and into the sunlight.

Payday started for her horse.

Doc said, "Where are you going?"

"I can't let him go by himself."

"You just told him it was a stupid idea. We all did."

"I know."

Doc grabbed her arm. "Let him go. He's stupid brave, and that's the worse kind."

"I know."

"He ain't really one of us, girl. He does good, that's great. We lose him, that's tough, but again, we've done fine with just us. Let him go if that's the way he wants it. I don't want to get too attached to him anyway. Just makes it harder. And listen, that two days left business, that's horse shit. He talks like a crazy man."

"A convincing crazy man," she said, but Payday relaxed and stared at the sunlight coming through the waterfall.

Smith rode Shadow into town slowly, making his way down Main Street. He took a dead cigar from his shirt pocket and lit it, reached back to one of his saddle bags and pulled out a stick of dynamite. He lit the dynamite off his cigar, tossed it into the open door of a looted store and rode on by. It exploded, knocking splintered pieces of wood and fragments of glass into the street behind him.

"Quill," he yelled. "Come out you lilly-livered sack of shit. The big boy sent me to take you home. Dead or alive."

He lit another stick of dynamite as he rode by Bessie's Clothes Emporium. He lit it, tossed it through a broken window and rode on to the next building, The Sundown Saloon.

"Shadow," he said, "before I blow this place down, I could use a drink."

Smith climbed down from Shadow and dropped the reins loosely over the hitching post, waiting a moment until the dynamite in Bessie's went off and blew most of the store into the street, along with clothes, shoes, and unmentionables, all of which fluttered about as if it were raining some kind of heavenly wardrobe.

"Long fuse," Smith said, looking back at the damage. He had learned by experience to prefer them.

He saw a green dress lying in the street. He sucked on his cigar, walked over and picked it up and looked at it. It wasn't burned, just knocked into the street. He picked it up and folded it and took it over to Shadow and folded it carefully and put it in a saddle bag.

Shadow made a snorting sound.

"It's all right, Shadow. It's not for me."

Smith reached into one of his saddle bags and pulled out a stick of dynamite, shoved it into his belt. He gently grasped the handles of his revolvers, raised them slightly and let them fall back smoothly into the holsters. He took another puff of his cigar and went into the saloon.

Inside he yelled out, "Quill! You in here? You awake yet? You piece of dog shit."

He made his way behind the bar, found a bottle of whisky, pulled the cork out with his teeth, drank from the bottle and looked at the beaded curtain. He stared at it for a moment, conjuring up memories of his previous life. He took another long drink from the bottle, put his cigar back in his mouth. He carried the bottle with him as he walked to the beaded curtain and pushed through, climbed the stairs, stopped on the landing, looked over the railing at the bottom floor of the saloon. He walked to the far end of the landing and tugged at the door there. It didn't budge, and then...

...for the first time in a long time, Smith felt a tinge of fear. It was such a rare feeling he had almost forgotten its true meaning. In fact, he had come to think it was something he no longer possessed. But now, the appearance of a shadow, a cold shadow falling across the landing, swelling, sent a tremor up his spine. His mind began to play with things unseen. He could smell it too. He could smell fear. His own fear. Inside of that smell was everything dark that he had ever feared as a child, as well as the darker realities of adulthood. The war and all the men and women he had killed, and even children, and knowing he was once that man, and maybe still was, compounded his feelings. Everything inside of him was raw. Smith wheeled toward the source of the shadow.

At the far end of the landing was Quill. Or what had once been Quill.

He crouched near the stairs clothed in a cold darkness. His teeth poked out of his mouth at all angles, his wings were spread, and beneath them shadows writhed. His ears had grown pointed and hairy. His face, chest, arms and legs, were covered in scales. His skull was knotted and there were knobs of bone on it. Two small horns projected from his forehead, one over the other. He stood on shiny black hooves, but as Smith stared at him, the hooves sprouted claws. His feet looked like the heads of ancient medieval weapons. He wore loose pants, and Smith remembered that he had been told he did that because he was in danger of snagging his johnson. Smith tried to keep that funny idea in mind to push back the fearful cold that was settling over him, pushing down deep into his bones like a cancer, but it didn't help much. A long, dark tail tipped with a spear-like point weaved in the air behind him. Like the hat and the pants, there was something humorous about that, but in the moment, Smith couldn't find a chuckle.

When Quill breathed out, his breath hissed across the landing. It was sour, almost poisonous. It made Smith wrinkle his nose and shut his mouth.

Quill stepped forward. His shadow swelled and dripped over the landing.

Smith thought for a moment his legs might buckle.

Quill opened his mouth, and a tongue to match the shape of his tail, flashed out and licked at the air, slapped over his lips, and went back inside his mouth. "You looking for me, cowboy?" Quill said.

It was all Smith could do to speak, but when he did it was without a hint of fear. His old nature had surfaced and pushed the fear back. It had to. It was the way he lived. Denying fear.

"Yep. I am looking for you. And for your information, we've met. But you weren't quite so ugly then. And you were Quill... How about now? Who are you? Quill? Or is it, Zelzarda?"

Smith thought Quill might spring at any moment, but instead he seemed to be relishing having trapped Smith on the landing. He seemed to relax. He was toying with Smith the way a cat toys with a mouse.

"My. You have friends in low places. They've given you a history lesson. But if you're what He's sent, then He's desperate. You have no idea what you're up against cowboy, and I don't think he does either. He always did underestimate me."

"I know about The Old Ones, and I know about the spell. I know what you want to do. I mean, really, pilgrim. Wouldn't you rather not make things so messy?"

"Even your employer preferred to rule in hell than serve in heaven. I'm no different."

"You're messing up the balance of things."

Quill hooded his eyes with eye-lids like scales, flicked them back open, dark and wide. "And you are going to set it right? For him? Is that what you think?"

"Bad as he is, he's a snappy dresser and a lot prettier than you."

Quill grinned his mouthful of teeth, took a step forward. Smith couldn't help himself. He took one step back.

Quill said, "You don't fool me."

"Who's foolin'?" Smith said.

"Do I sense fear?"

"Caution," Smith said. "You sense caution. I was a little puckered in the ass there for a minute, but now I'm fine. I'm all right."

"Fear is what I sense."

"You sense shit. I got you right where I want you."

This statement caused Quill to show all his saliva-wet teeth again. A rumbling that might have been intestinal disturbance or laughter churned up from his stomach and bellowed out of his mouth, riding on stink.

When Quill quit laughing, he said, "Now that you've found me, what are you going to do with me?"

Smith dropped the whisky bottle, drew both revolvers and fired a shot from each. The shots hit Quill in the teeth, knocking his head back and the bullets ricocheting off into the rickety lumber that made up the saloon.

Quill snapped his head back into position. His teeth sizzled and smoked. "Enough." Quill said, wheeled and slammed his fist down on the stair railing so hard the railing cracked, and then Quill kicked back at the stairway. Steps screeched as nails tore loose and the stairs smashed on the barroom floor.

"No way out," Quill said.

Smith opened up with both revolvers. He hit Quill in the chest, shot after shot. Quill staggered back, injured by the special loads, but not put down. Quill roared. His wings more flailed than flapped as they smashed against the wall, knocking part of it down, tearing the stair railing apart on one side, sending pieces of it clattering to the floor below.

Quill let out a kind of screech, jerked a piece of the railing loose, threw it at Smith, hit him hard in the chest and knocked him back against the wall, on his butt, jarring the cigar loose from his jaws. Smith still clutched one of his revolvers, but the other was knocked free and went tumbling to a table below, bounced off of it, hit the floor and slid against the bar.

Payday came into the saloon. She saw Smith's revolver on the floor, heard the commotion upstairs. She picked up the revolver, glanced up and saw Smith lying against the wall, one leg dangling through what was left of the railing. And across from him, moving slowly toward him like a snake toward its prey was Quill. She was shocked at Quill's appearance.

She thought she could no longer be shocked, but he was bigger and uglier and stranger than ever before.

"Smith," she yelled.

Smith was working himself to his feet, his back still against the wall. "Kind of busy right now," he said.

Quill had paused to pluck the silver loads from his chest. He pinched out the flattened silver. It hissed and smoked between his thumb and forefinger. He dropped it to the floor.

"A minor inconvenience," Quill said.

Smith fired again, but the hammer snapped on an empty chamber. "Damn," he said, scrambled to reload from his belt. His fingers fumbled because Quill was rushing toward him. No more cat and mouse. It was done.

There was a popping sound of gunfire. Quill grabbed at his crotch and staggered. It was Payday, firing from below with Smith's revolver.

Smith jerked the stick of dynamite from his belt, held it over the side of the railing.

"Payday. Light it!"

She fired, using Smith's revolver.

The wick sizzled.

Quill looked at the dynamite, made a face like a man with his jaws packed full of lemons.

Smith tossed it at Quill, said, "Catch," and leaped off the landing, twisted and fell on his back against the table below, just as the dynamite went off and the world became a loud explosion and a mass of flying debris.

(2)

ayday found herself in the street with ringing ears and a splinter in her ass. She rolled over, plucked out the splinter, and limped back toward what was left of the saloon; a bit of the building's frame, the bar, and even a shelf of whisky.

Something moved in the rubble.

Smith raised his head. He still had his hat on, but the sides of it were pushed down over his ears and it was dripping fragments of lumber, sawdust, and dirt. Payday made her way to him, lifted him up, and draped one of her arms under one of his.

"You all right?" she said.

"Except for the falling part."

Out in the street they saw that the hitching post had been blasted off at the supports. Payday's horse and Shadow had dragged it into the street. Smith called Shadow up, and the black stallion came forward, pulling the post between his legs, dragging Payday's horse along with him.

"Did we get him?" Smith said.

A geyser of debris and dust rose up where the center of the saloon had been. A wing flapped out of the dust. There was a screeching like a thousand pigs being dripped in hot water, and then the demon rose up a few feet into the air and fell down again, on its knees. His body bent. He shook his head.

Payday worked the horses reins loose from the post. She swung into her saddle, said, "Nope. Looks pretty spry. Let's get the hell out of here."

In the next moment, Smith was on Shadow, and they were riding fast, side by side down Main Street, heading for anyplace but there.

Birds in the hundreds rose up startled from hideouts in abandoned buildings, rose up high and black and squawking, filled the sky so thoroughly it looked for a moment like a rain cloud. Their shadows blackened the street briefly, and then they were gone, leaving hot sunlight in place of their darkness.

They were riding close. Payday said, "You didn't kill him, but you gave him pause."

"Silver in the dynamite stick," Smith said. "Dug some out of the cave walls, poked a lot of pieces of it into the stick. It didn't do what I hoped it would do, but it got his attention."

Smith lingered on that thought. He had managed to bring the big guy out into the open by seeming to be careless, thinking Quill wouldn't know what he had in store for him—the silver. That part had worked. The silver had hurt the monster, but it hadn't stopped him. Smith had thought if he hit him with enough of it, it would take him down. At this point, Smith was uncertain anything could stop him. With or without his minions, the old boy was a full load of bad business. Smith had gained greater respect for the monster's power. But he knew one thing for sure. The silver bothered him.

(3)

A wing flexed. Dust puffed. Quill stood, disturbing broken lumber at his feet.

He looked at the sky and swelled his chest and flexed his muscles. Little silver fragments that had been stuffed in the dynamite popped out of his body like dollops of hot grease.

There were holes in his wings. One of his eyes was an empty gap. Teeth had been blown out of his mouth. He turned his head toward the ground and strained and the ground shook and the air quivered, and slowly, the holes in his wings began to fill. A replacement for his missing eye swelled within him, poked into the socket and filled the gap. Teeth sprouted like ripe plants where before there were only nubs and holes and spaces. The old broken teeth fell out of his mouth and tinkled onto the burnt and blasted lumber at his feet. He flexed his wings and rose into the sky, his tail rising behind him like a flag. He darted over Main Street, over the buildings. He saw dust where Shadow and Payday's horse had gone. He went in that direction, but soon there were thick trees and the ground was no longer visible and there was no more tell-tale dust.

Quill lowered himself, flew beneath tree level, dodging between tree trunks with dexterity and speed, watching.

Payday led Smith to a place in the midst of the trees. There was hard rock under the trees and there was a soft spot where the tall pines had dropped their needles. Roots from the trees had heaved the rocks, causing some of them to poke up like miniature tombstones. She dismounted, squatted, found a flat stretch beneath the trees, felt under the pine needles, got hold of the edge of something, and pulled it up.

It was a huge trap door. When she had it lifted, she took a long board from a groove in the side of the opening, put it under the trap door at the edge to hold it up. There was a slanting, boarded path that led down into the darkness. She went inside and the darkness swallowed her up. Smith waited with the horses. Payday reappeared with a lit lantern.

"The horses can come down," she said.

Smith led the horses after Payday. When they were inside she showed him a place where he could tie them up, then she removed the board prop and let the trap door fall into place, leaving them with golden lantern light and the smell of horse sweat. The place was simple, some barrels, a bench, and two caskets on saw horses. Great tree roots twisted and webbed in the dirt and rock walls.

"What is this place?" Smith asked.

"Undertaker kept his caskets down here," she said.

"Why?"

"I'm not sure, but I think it's because he liked to come here and have privacy. He made the caskets himself. He put a trap door on this hole, and he had his own sanctuary. Since this old cavern wasn't well known, it was a place where he could have peace and quiet. I don't think it was any more than that. He made it a hideaway. First place I hid out after Doc fixed me up. Later we moved from here to the cave. That way we weren't so close to Quill. The one behind the waterfall is safer, but this place will do. The trap door is tight enough to keep the light from showing, but it's best we move farther in, so sound won't carry."

"He finds out we're here, we'd be trapped like rats in a box."

"Not exactly," Payday said, carrying the lantern, starting to walk into the darkness at the rear of the hideaway. "There's another way out, a back tunnel and another trap door. The horses can't get through that one though. But right now, I'm tuckered, and my ears are still ringing from that dynamite blast. Come on." They moved back into the cavern by means of a natural rock tunnel, came to another wide spot. Payday placed the lantern on a metal hook that had been driven into the rock wall. There were a couple of small barrels. Payday rolled one over for Smith, one for herself. She handed Smith his pistol.

"Thought you might want that back."

Thanks," Smith said, then sitting on a barrel, he said, "What's in these?"

"They're empty," she said.

"Why did you help me out back there? I thought you didn't care for me much."

"Been asking myself the same question," she said. "I guess because you're human and he isn't. And you seemed genuinely interested in my welfare back at the cave. And hell, I think you're an idiot, but you got the same enemies we do."

"I may not be as human as you think," Smith said.

"All right. Real reason? I think you might be of some help to us, if you live long enough."

"That sounds more honest," Smith said. "But for whatever reason you showed up, I'm beholden. One thing I'm curious about. When you shot up through the landing, how did you know where Quill was standing?"

"I didn't."

"You could have shot me," Smith said.

"Could have worked out that way, but it didn't. I considered his size and weight, because the landing was sagging there, and decided it was him."

"What if you were wrong?" he said.

"Then we wouldn't be having this conversation. Okay, truth. I could see you and him clearly from my angle."

"You just wanted to pull my leg."

"I did. Do you still think you can kill Quill alone?"

"I'm considerably less confident," Smith said. "I was full of piss and vinegar this morning, now I feel like I'm mostly full of hot air. Doesn't usually work out against me when it comes to gunplay and rough stuff. I guess in time all things change. Like right now, I'm feeling tired and old and whipped."

Payday leaned over and looked at Smith. "You got a pretty nasty wound there. And you're bleeding through your shirt."

"Like Humpy Dumpty, I had a great fall."

"Lets see if we can put you together again," she said. "Take off your shirt. I think Undertaker has some of his whisky hidden around here somewhere, or most everywhere."

Smith started removing his shirt. Payday strolled back into the darker part of the hollow, came back with a little bottle of whisky. "Pure-Dee rot-gut," she said.

"I could use a drink," Smith said.

"Not what I had in mind," Payday said.

Payday saw in the lantern light that Smith's muscular body was pocked and striped with scars, as well as the fresh wounds.

"My," she said, "with the light just right, you look like a man prone to accidents."

"I've had my share," he said. "I've sort of been pieced back together, you might say."

Payday unscrewed the bottle cap and poured a bit of whisky on the wound, took a shot herself.

"How about me?" Smith said.

"If you must," she said, and handed him the bottle. He took a swig. When he lowered the bottle he saw that Payday was staring at him.

"What?"

"You can't be him," she said. "But you remind me of him. The look in your eye. The dynamite. But you can't be him... Here. Put more whisky on it. That's all we got. But it might help it to not become infected."

Smith pulled his shirt back on, found a fragment of a cigar in his pocket, along with matches, and lit up. He took a deep drag.

"Did you ever have a moustache?" she asked.

"I've been known to wear one."

"He was older."

"Payday, you got the right man," Smith said. "I am who you think I am. Or I was. But not now. The fellow you knew was blown to hell. And I do mean that exactly."

Payday stepped back, shook her head. "You can't be. A younger brother, maybe. A cousin, but not him."

"I'm him, I'm sorry to say."

"If you are, I ought to kill you... If a bullet would do it."

"It will do it, and you probably should shoot me. I won't even keep you from it."

"You son-of-a-bitch," she said, and a tear trickled down her face. She drew her revolver and pointed it at him. "You didn't even try to help."

"I know," he said.

Smith didn't move. He didn't so much as blink.

"You didn't help me," she said. "Quill did this to me, and you were there, and you didn't help me."

Smith nodded. "I should have. But I didn't. I would now."

"Now doesn't do me a lot of good, does it?" Payday said. "Now won't give me my eye back. You think an apology would make it all right? Like you stepped on my toe... Wait a minute, you can't be him. You were blown up."

Smith nodded.

"You are him. I know you are. You don't look like him, yet you do. Somehow, you're him."

"Yep," Smith said. "And I'm not apologizing. That would be pointless. You can pull the trigger, and I wouldn't blame you. I'm back for a reason. I'm back to stop Quill. I can't do it by myself. I know that now. But he can be stopped. I have to believe that, and I have to believe that with your help, and your friends, we can do it. When it's all done, I'll stand right in front of you and let you pull the trigger."

"You're here now and I can pull the trigger," she said.

"True enough," he said.

Payday studied Smith for a long time. Slowly she lowered the hammer on her revolver and put it away. "If you really are him, and I find that hard to accept, I think I'm making a mistake by not blowing a hole in you."

"I'll try to prove to you that you aren't," Smith said. "I was that man, but I'm not him now. That's all I know to say, and I know that doesn't help much."

"You're right. It doesn't."

They waited down there for a time, and while they waited they sat in silence, until Smith finally said, "Where did you learn to use that whip, shoot like that?"

"So now it's small talk. You caused me to lose my eye. Remember. We discussed this."

"I know. And me saying over and over again that the old me isn't the new me doesn't matter."

"Do people really change?"

"All the time, but most, not much. But then I've had a kind of death experience."

Payday studied Smith's face. "You look the same, and yet you don't."

"You've said that. I'm telling you, hard as it is to believe, the old me is dead. I'm the new me. I'm trying to start fresh by saving the world."

Payday actually smiled at that comment. "Not that it's any of your business, but I learned it from my Pa. We had a traveling sharp-shooting and trick-riding show. I got better than my ma, who was the original trick-shooter and whip-mistress, so I took her place. I was twelve. The whip I learned from Ma. That was her thing. I took to it like a fish to water. When I was thirteen she got sick and died. Then it was just me and Pa.

"Pa took to drinking too much, and one day when he was drunk, three hombres robbed us and killed Pa. When they got through with me, they sold me to a whorehouse in Mexico. Got sold again by that house three years later to one in Arizona. I didn't have any fire left after that. Didn't care if I lived or died. Then one day one of the men who sold me showed up. I'd grown some, of course. He didn't recognize me. I got hold of his own gun and shot him in the balls, stole his horse, and lit out.

"I decided to look for the other two. Never found them. Lucky them. I tried to catch on with a wild west show, but never did, and wound up in Falling Rock. I needed to eat, and I needed a roof over my head, so I took up my other trade. The one those men had taught me. You know the rest. Or all you need to know."

"My story isn't a lot different."

"You were a whore?"

"No. But I got left for dead on the family farm in Missouri. Five Yankee soldiers killed my ma and pa and my two brothers. I took a shot to the head. Grazed me, put me out. I was twelve, same as you were when you had your bad break. I came awake later and my family was gone. It soured me. By the time I was seventeen I was riding with Quantrail and the James brothers. The hate kept building. Always had it in the back of my mind what those Yankees done to my family. Never caught them, but the need to festered until I didn't care about anything or anybody. You witnessed that man. It's different now."

"Like I said, I'm not sure people really change all that much," she said.

"Yet, you came to help me."

"I didn't know who you were."

"But you had suspicions, right?"

"It didn't make any sense though."

"After all you've seen it should. Quill. Trapped inside this big chunk of country. Not being able to ride out of it. And you think me coming back from the dead, having transformed myself is impossible? Remember. No one in that saloon but a woman came to your aid. You're with some of those same people now everyday. Why pick me as the worst one there?"

Payday didn't respond, but Smith could see he had touched on something. He decided to leave it at that, hope his actions would speak louder than his words.

"I'm tired," he said.

Smith took off his gun belt and draped it over a chair. He laid down on top of a coffin lid. Payday's attention was drawn to his holstered revolvers. In the weak light the silver bullets in Smith's gun belt gleamed like stars.

Smith lay silent with his eyes closed. Payday sat and watched him sleep for a long time. Finally, gently, she pulled her pistol, cocked it and aimed it. Her hand trembled a little.

"Get that light, will you?" Smith said without opening his eyes.

Payday hesitated a moment.

Smith opened his eyes then, said, "The light."

Payday put her pistol away, picked up her whip, snapped it at the candle, flicked out the light.

(4)

A few hours later the horses became restless, began to stir and snort. Smith got up, struck a match and lit the candle.

Smith picked up his gun belt and put it on. He looked at Payday. She was sitting on the ground in a corner, her back against the wall.

"I need to get you back to the cave," Smith said. "We have the cover of night now."

"So suddenly you're protecting me?"

"Better late than never, I suppose."

"I can take care of myself just fine. Hell, I saved your ass."

"You did at that. So now we're a team."

"You keep thinking that."

"Main thing is I want to go back, make preparations. I admit doing this alone is over my head. And frankly, I'm kind of on a time schedule."

Payday stood up and opened the hideaway. They led their horses out of it, and then Smith helped her close the hideout trap door, kick pine straw over it. It was night now, and moon-bright. They rode their horses into the moonlight. When they arrived at the road, Smith reined his horse to a stop, turned in the saddle and looked back at the town. Falling Rock was some distance away, but he could clearly see the bell tower. It was tall and it blocked a view of the moon. Moon beams split against the tower, forked out on either side.

"The two moons," Smith said. "Now I get it."

When Smith and Payday failed to return, Undertaker and Doc went searching, Doc on horseback, Undertaker in his little wagon, clattering more than was cautious down the dusty road. The night was rich with sweet air, and the moonlight gave the trees shadows that draped across the road like crow wings.

"Anything happens to that girl I'll cut the rest of your legs off," Doc said.

"How the hell is this my fault?" Undertaker said. "She's a big girl. You didn't try and stop her. She can handle herself better than we do."

"Then why are we looking for her if we're so sure she can?"

"You're the one's all fired up. She's probably back at the cave eating a hot meal, which is what we ought to be doing. We can't run around after her like we're her daddy. And out here, like this, it's stupid."

"Well, here we are. So be alert."

"I'm always alert," Undertaker said. "I was born alert. My mama used to say if there was one thing I was it was alert. My goddamn middle name is alert."

"So, you've noticed that there's a ghoul on a horse behind us?" Undertaker said.

"Don't mess with me."

"Really, Mr. Alert. There's a ghoul."

That's when Undertaker heard a horse's hooves behind him, turned to look. There was indeed a ghoul, riding behind them at a trot. The hat the ghoul wore had fallen below where his ears used to be, and to compensate the ghoul had pushed the brim back in front. There was very little flesh on his face, and his neck was nearly all bone held together by dark, rotting meat.

"Shit," Undertaker said.

Another ghoul rode out of the forest at the edge of the road and fell in beside the other. This one looked a little fresher. The horse didn't.

"You need to write your mama," Doc said, "and tell her you're going to have to have your middle name changed to Not So Alert."

Two more ghouls on horseback drifted off a forest trail and onto the road, quite close to Doc and Undertaker. It was Gene and Roy. The four ghouls started to pick up speed.

Undertaker glanced back, said, "On the count of three. Three!"

Away they went in a burst of dust and a clatter of hooves and behind them rode the ghouls, yelling and gaining ground. A bullet whizzed between Doc and Undertaker.

"To hell with this," said Undertaker. He clucked to his horse, wheeled away from Doc, turned his rig, and went charging right at the ghouls. He lifted one of his bottle bombs and lit it with a snap of a match. He did it without any effort, reins in his teeth, bottle in one hand, match in the other, brought the match to fiery light with a cut of his thumb nail. The oiled rag jutting out of the bottle took the flame instantly.

Undertaker rode toward the ghouls and tossed the bottle, hitting Bony Neck square in the face. The bottle burst and the contents blazed and lapped around the ghoul's face, causing him to become a living candle. The living candle hurtled from horseback and splattered in the road, dead flesh and rotten bones shattering like a glass cup. Even his horse had caught on fire, its rotten bones ripe for kindling. The horse collapsed slowly, like the timbers of a building coming undone.

Roy and Gene jerked their horses wide, but the remaining ghoul held his ground, pulled his pistol, and fired as he passed Undertaker. The shot struck the old man in the side, causing him to drop a second bottle he had just lit right into his lap.

"Aw hell," Undertaker said.

The bottle exploded, a great tongue of fire licked over Undertaker, gathered him up in a bloom of flame. He tried to scream, but the flames rushed down his throat and waved out of his nostrils. The rig began to burn and the horses bolted, pulling after them a chariot of fire. They had only gone a short distance when the main part of the rig came apart and collapsed in the road. The horse rushed on, pulling bits of the wagon after them.

By this time Doc had whipped about and was riding to Undertaker, a pistol in one hand, firing as fast as he could pull the trigger, hitting the ghoul that had shot Undertaker three times in the chest. Even as the ghoul grinned, rode hard toward him, thinking the shots weren't going to bother him, his chest wounds began to widen and sizzle.

"Dagnabit," the ghoul said, and fell apart on horseback, splattered in the road, sliding and slipping apart on dirt and gravel. The dead horse galloped past Doc and charged off into the night.

"Silver bullets, asshole," Doc said to the dissolving corpse. He had just that day prepared them. They were cruder than Smith's, just slices in the lead, bits of silver pushed in, and the lead molded back over it. But it worked. He shot the rider's horse in the head, and the silver worked there as well.

A bullet hit Doc in the arm, sent his pistol flying. Gene and Roy were on either side of him, their pistols leveled at him.

"You might want to hold up there and just enjoy the fire," Gene said to Doc. "It's a little warm to get up too close, but it is pretty, don't you think?"

Gene snatched the reins of Doc's mount from his hand, held them.

"You smell meat cooking, Gene?" Roy said, riding close on Doc's other side.

"I do," Gene said. "Makes me hungry. Course, I'm always hungry. Cooked or raw, young or old, man, woman, child, or little kitty cat. I'm always ready to eat."

Doc swallowed, glanced at his old friend. He was nothing more than a blackened chunk of sizzling meat and snapping bone, mixed in with the charred rig.

"You spawns of hell," Doc said, holding his arm tight to contain the flow of blood.

"Well now," Gene said. "That's mighty harsh language from our soon-to-be dessert. We eat the grilled fellow first, and then you get to be a pie or some such. We might even eat your horse, we're hungry enough."

Roy snickered. "Yeah, old man, we're gonna eat you alive. Start with some soft parts, work our way inside to the warm, sweet guts. It'll be a lot of fun. For us."

With a yell, Doc dug his heels into his horse's flanks, caused it to smash into Gene's horse and knock Gene off, dropping him on his ass in the middle of the road.

"You old son-of-a-bitch," Gene said, as he picked up his pistol, scrambled to his feet.

A light streaked through the night and a flaming arrow lodged itself in the back of Gene's head. Gene straightened up, and then the flames flashed up and caught his hat and scraggly hair on fire.

"What the hell?" Gene said.

"Your head's on fire," Roy said.

Flames coiled around Gene's skull, and then Gene's rotten head popped open, his blackened brain oozed out like watery dung, and he fell over, his head consumed with fire. An arrow hit the horse in the head, and down it went, flames whipping along its rotten head and causing it to stagger and fall and burn.

Another blazing arrow whizzed past Doc and hit Roy firmly in the chest.

Roy snatched at the arrow, breaking it off. He slapped the flames crawling across his shirt. Another arrow whizzed past his ear. Roy reined his horse around, popped its butt with his pistol barrel, galloped away at a dead run.

Doc saw three men standing by the side of the road. He was relieved, and surprised to see they weren't ghouls. It was the cocky kid, Double Shot, and an Indian in leather leggings and loose leather shirt. The Kid and Double Shot had torches, the Indian a quiver full of arrows, and a bow that he was slipping over one shoulder. His clothes were a mixture of Indian leather and white man goods, including a red neckerchief. The Indian's hair was in braids wrapped in tatters of an American flag.

There was a clatter of hooves behind Doc. He turned, expecting the worst.

It was Smith and Payday.

All of them stopped near Undertaker's wagon. Payday dismounted, trembling. She stood looking at the wagon and Undertaker's remains. He looked like nothing more than a bunch of blackened sticks.

"I shouldn't have left him," she said, and she almost sagged to the ground.

Doc and Smith climbed down from their horses. The Kid, Double Shot, and the Indian stood nearby, watching the burning corpse.

Doc touched Payday's shoulder, said, "He knew the chances same as you. Nothing could have been done. It happened quick and it was over, in the time it took me to turn my horse around."

"I'm going back," Payday said, wheeling about, taking hold of her horse's reins. "I'm going back, and I'm going to kill Quill."

"That's a good idea," Smith said grabbing her arm. "A real good idea. We all want to kill him. And we will. But not right now. Not yet. I learned my lesson today, and it's a lesson you already know. I should have listened. It will take all of us. Together."

(5)

The Kid, Double Shot and the Indian had horses tied off in the woods. They got them, and they all rode together to the waterfall and the cave. As they dismounted inside, locked the horses in the makeshift corral and lit the torches along the wall, Payday paused to roll Doc's sleeve up and look at his arm.

"Shot went all the way through," she said.

"You can use some whisky out of my bag to sterilize the wound, and I can use a little to sterilize my throat."

Payday brought Doc the whisky. He took a hit before pouring some on his arm.

While this was going on The Kid kept staring at Smith, watching the torch light flicker across his face. He reached out and grabbed Smith's arm.

"That's not a good habit, Kid," Smith said.

"I know who you are. I don't know how it's you, but it is. It's you, prettied up some, but it's you. I don't forget someone did to me what you did."

"You're observant. That's a good quality. Most of the time."

"How can it be?" The Kid said.

"Don't figure on it, it'll hurt your head."

"I seen it was you back there in the firelight. I knew it right off, but I couldn't accept it. I couldn't figure it. I still don't figure it, but I know sure as shit stinks, it's you."

"Let it go, boy," Smith said. "You're only part right."

The Kid stepped back a pace. "I can't allow insults like you gave me to pass. I just can't. Even if you and me are on the same side now."

The others were watching all this quietly until Payday said, "I wouldn't do that, Kid."

"After what he didn't do for you, you can say that," The Kid said.

"He's the same, but he isn't."

"The same and he isn't?" The Kid said. "What the hell does that mean?"

"It means some things are beyond explaining. I have reasons to hate him more than you, but... He's not the same."

The Kid studied Smith. "That's ridiculous. Putting on clean clothes and shaving doesn't change the asshole in the pants. And I can tell you one thing right fast fella. You're going to pay. I don't forgive so easy."

"I haven't forgiven him anything," Payday said. "But if I can stand him, so can you."

The cocky kid grinned. "Tell you what I'm going to do big man. I'm going to—"

Smith jerked his pistol loose, stepped forward briskly and whacked The Kid a solid one across the forehead. The Kid folded and lay on the ground like a pile of dropped laundry. The Indian snickered.

"They can't be good for his head," Payday said.

"It's better than a bullet," Smith said.

Doc bent down and looked at the knot on The Kid's forehead, checked his pulse. "He'll live, but he'll have one hell of a headache. If he stays around you better watch your back, Smith. And maybe you ought to explain what's going on here. What he said. What Payday said. I'm not sure I get it."

"I prefer to let that lay for now," Smith said.

"You keep letting it lay," Doc said.

"It's best," Payday said. "I don't even understand what I know about it."

Doc nodded. "Very well." He turned to Double Shot. "Good to see you and The Kid alive. How does the Indian fit in the picture?"

"He's been with us awhile, him and some of his people," Double Shot said. "Let him tell you. He speaks American. Sort of."

"Speak good American," the Indian said, sitting on the ground, crossing his legs. "Speak better Shoshone."

"I speak both," Payday said. "I speak American better."

The Indian shrugged. "My name Cameahwait. Priest name me William Brown. Bad name for Shoshone." He turned to Payday, said, "I speak you Shoshone. You tell what say American."

"I think I can do that," Payday said.

Cameahwait began to tell his story while Smith built a fire and put on a pot of beans. The Kid had not moved.

By the time the beans were bubbling, Cameahwait had finished his tale. Payday nodded at him, spoke a few words in Shoshone, turned to the others. "I'll tell you what he told me as best I can. He's the last of his band.

What white men call a chief, though the Shoshone don't see it that way. A leader among leaders might be the best way to describe it. No one has to follow him, but if they like what he has to say, and he proves himself though deeds, then they follow. His group were holed up in a mine in Pine Canyon, about two miles from here. He was there with his daughter, her husband, two old braves and a white woman whose head had flown South. That's what he said. I think he's trying to say she was crazy. That's how it translated to me, but understand, I'm no expert in Shoshone.

"He was protecting her because she couldn't figure which shoe goes on which foot. He felt sorry for her. She went loco when she saw her family killed and eaten by ghouls. She felt guilty because she was hiding under her cabin, saw it happen through the floorboards. She said nothing, did nothing, just lay there and looked up through the cracks and watched them die. Their blood dripped through the cracks onto her face, and she did nothing. Cameahwait thinks there was nothing she could do, but she felt otherwise and went loco. Cameahwait and his band got so hungry they were eating roots and bark from some old trees near the mine. One day they all ventured out, hoping to kill game, find food, but he and his band got jumped by ghouls. He lost all of his people. Barely escaped himself. He says, like the crazy woman, he went a little loco himself. He hid out and went out from time to time and killed ghouls with his arrows. Once he learned you had to shoot them in the head or burn them, he did all right. He was fighting his own war. And then he found Double Shot and his partner, hiding out in the forest, living close to the edge themselves. They banded together for the last few days, were staying in the mine with him."

"It ain't much of a place," Double Shot said. "In its day, however, all that silver runs through it could have made a man rich. But we were getting mighty hungry there. It ain't a place near much game, that's for sure. Only thing grows around there is rocks, so you can't even find a dandelion green to eat. Nothing. That's why we were out in the woods tonight. We had traveled some distance from the mine. We were looking for food. That's when we saw the fire...Undertaker burning."

Payday took a deep breath, and her eyes welled with tears. "Poor Undertaker."

"There was nothing that could be done," Doc said.

"You keep saying that," Payday said, wiping her arm across her eyes.

"Because it's true," Doc said.

The Kid had begun to snore.

(6)

They built a fire and settled down by it to eat their dinner. The Kid had finally come awake, and he was feeling anything but frisky. He sat up and rubbed his head and watched Smith eat. While The Kid had lain unconscious, Smith had taken his guns and put them away. Smith looked up at The Kid a couple of times, but otherwise acted as if nothing had happened.

Double Shot finished eating and opened up a flask of whisky. Doc watched him, said, "You know, you don't mind, I'd like a shot of that."

Double Shot hesitated. "I thought you might be past it... You know?"

"Being a drunk?" Doc said.

"Close enough."

"Come on, give me a jolt," Doc said.

Double Shot passed the flask to Doc, and just as Doc was about to take it in his hand, Smith said, "You know, Doc, you've been looking pretty good with your face held high."

"You have," Payday said.

"First time I seen you your face was on a table and you were drunk as a tick in whisky barrel," The Kid said.

Everyone looked at The Kid. It was the first thing he had said since being whacked in the head by Smith. "I mean, I ain't one to judge a man one way or the other, but I'm going to ride with someone, deal with what we're dealing with, I'd prefer they be sober. Especially if they got a problem with their liquor."

Doc moved his hand away from the extended flask. "Maybe later," he said. "I ain't feeling as thirsty as I was."

Doc got up and walked off into the shadows at the rear of the cave.

When he was gone, Payday said, "That was good of you, Smith. And you too, Kid. He hasn't been drinking as much, but tonight, with Undertaker dead, I think he might have wanted to have him a real blind-ass toot."

Double Shot looked at the fire. "Hell, I was going to give him a jolt. But I'm glad he didn't take it."

"Just a thought, Double Shot," Smith said, "but if you could keep that flask out of sight when you're around Doc, it would help him out, and like The Kid said, in the long run, we're going to ride with a man, it would be best he wasn't falling off a horse. For extra measure, you might want to pull back on that stuff yourself. Everyone needs to keep a clear head."

Double Shot nodded and put the flask away inside his coat pocket, did it as gently as if he were putting a child to bed.

After awhile The Kid said to Smith, "You gonna give me my guns back?"

"Not tonight. Not while you might still be in the mood to cause trouble."

"I might could get another gun," The Kid said.

"You might," Smith said.

The Kid turned away and said no more. After awhile they all turned in. Smith found a place in the back of the cave, off in a tunnel. He laid his bed roll there. He wrapped The Kid's pistols in his coat and laid it aside. He pulled off his boots and was about to slip under his blankets, when Payday showed up. He couldn't see her clearly, only her shape, and behind her, down the length of the tunnel he could see wisps of the fire still blazing, its light protected from outside view by the cave and the waterfall. The smoke from it was drifting into the falling water, dissipating.

"You could have killed Jimmy, but you didn't," Payday said.

"Jimmy?"

"That's The Kid's name. Jimmy."

"Suits him," Smith said.

"Maybe you have changed," she said.

"Let's just say I had a real strong outside influence to do better, and leave it at that."

"I don't know why, but I believe you. You won't let me down will you? You won't make me feel like a fool?"

"I'll sure try not to."

She moved to him and it happened smoothly, the way water flowed, or the sun rose, natural and straight away without delay. He took her in his arms, and their lips met. They kissed for awhile. Smith reached up and touched her eye patch. She grabbed his hand.

"I'm...I'm so ugly."

He slipped it off her face. He could see a bit of what had been done to her in the shadows. He said, "You're beautiful."

"Once," she said.

"More now than ever, I'm sure."

They eased onto the bed roll, melted together like butter on a stove. The fire at the front of the cavern died down and darkness crawled over them.

(7)

In the morning before the sun was up, Smith awoke with Payday lying in the crook of his arm, which had gone to sleep from the pressure. He slipped out from under the blankets silently, and removed the green dress from his saddlebag. He laid it out beside her, dressed, and walked to where the fire had been, and built it up again.

When he had it going, he took off his shirt, went to the waterfall and dipped his hands in it and splashed his face and washed the water over his chest. It was cold and it made him shiver, but it was a good feeling too. He went to the edge of the waterfall and worked himself along the border of the falls where it was dry and stepped outside. The sun was coming up. He watched until it was bright and clear and the air was clean and brisk. A soft wind rustled the leaves in the trees. Smith could see the dew on the bits of grass that hadn't wilted from the cold night, and the rocks along the stream glistened with it, and the water was a sparkly blue band. For a moment it was easy to forget things were so topsy-turvy. It wasn't the world as he had known it, but maybe for him it could be better. Perhaps he was giving himself too much credit. Perhaps a whiff of brimstone had done little more than clean up his face and part his hair, and in time he'd go back to being who he was before.

No. He wouldn't. He couldn't. Not after last night with Payday. Now he not only owed it to himself to be better than he was, he owed it to her. He owed it to everybody was the way he saw it.

Smith took a deep breath of the crisp air, went back inside the cave, put his shirt on and started breakfast, letting his damp skin dry against the shirt. Breakfast was a simple thing to do, put on a pot of beans and roll out some biscuits with the sourdough starter, put them in the Dutch oven, and set it on the coals. He used a small camp shovel to put coals on top of the oven so the biscuits would cook more evenly.

When beans and biscuits were cooking, he went back to his bedroll and got his hat and guns, and he got The Kid's guns. He slung them over his shoulder. He did all of this without waking Payday.

He slipped back to the front of the cave, squatted by the fire and used a big wooden spoon that had come from someone in their group, and stirred the beans. He stuck the coffee pot into the falls and filled it with water, found damp coffee grounds in a somewhat moldy leather bag by the cave wall. He had seen Doc pour grounds out of it before. The grounds smelled like sweat and leather. He mixed them in the water in the coffee pot. It would make thin coffee, but it was some kind of coffee. When the water was boiling and the smell of coffee was filling the cave, The Kid woke up and came over. He squatted to the right of Smith. He saw his holster and guns on a rock.

The Kid said, "Those are my guns."

"They are at that," Smith said.

"Any chance I can have them back?"

"Any chance you're going to shoot me?"

The Kid was silent for awhile. He said, "What say we call it a truce until we get done with what we're doing?"

"And how do we know when that's done?" Smith asked.

"I'll let you say."

"And if I don't say?"

"Maybe I'll say."

"And maybe we can forget the whole thing if I apologize, say I'm sorry?"

"For both times you hit me?"

"Both times."

The Kid contemplated, said, "Payday trusts you."

"Does that help you like me any better?"

"I don't know, but it makes me think on it a little," The Kid said.

"I'm not going to keep harping on this, as I've done that enough. I'm going to say it again, though, and then I'm going to shut up about it. I'm not the same as I was. It's important to me you know that. It's even more important I know that, but I can only say it so many times."

"Not sure I can sort that out," The Kid said.

Smith grunted, slipped the gun belt and pistols off the rock and tossed them to the kid. "Let's just start with mutual trust."

"Fair enough," The Kid said, catching the gun belt.

When The Kid had the belt on, Smith picked up a metal cup and poured coffee in it. He said, "You want to try it? The name's Jimmy, right?"

"That's right."

"Kid Jimmy," Smith said.

"No one calls me that."

"I do. At least once."

Jimmy took the cup offered him, sipped, frowned. "It's not very good. But you know what, it'll do."

Before long everyone was up. The aroma of Smith's biscuits, beans and coffee had pulled them from sleep. They sat and ate. Payday leaned toward Smith, said, "I have no place to wear that dress."

"Put it up. Maybe the time will come."

"It's nice."

"I don't want to spoil the moment, but it didn't cost me anything."

Double Shot said, "I got to go piss."

"You don't need to keep us informed," Doc said.

"It's important to me," Double Shot said, "so I think it should be important to others."

Cameahwait snickered.

Double Shot went outside the water fall to find his place. He came back swiftly.

"Trouble?" Smith said, standing up.

"Not the sort you're thinking," Double Shot said. "Unless I passed out and don't remember, I thought it was morning."

That's when a shadow crept along the waterfall and the fire seemed brighter.

"The moon is coming up," Double Shot said.

They all went outside. Part of the sky had grown dark, and the dark was spreading, like spilled ink easing over a bright blotter. The moon was up, riding high, full and bright as a polished concho. There was a sound in the heavens like something groaning, like heavy machinery slowly coming apart.

"Not good," Cameahwait said.

"It's happening," Smith said.

"What's happening?" The Kid said. "What the hell is going on?"

"The Old Ones," Smith said. "The Long Dark Night."

"Who are they?" Double Shot said. "And what's the Long Dark Night?"

Smith said, "For right now just think BAD. Ready or not, we have to make our play. This is our last day, our last shot."

Back inside, by the fire, Smith pinched silver loads from his gun belt, gave them each one bullet, said, "Take the shells you have out, put one of these in your gun belt, and you'll never run out. They are deadly to the ghouls, less so to Quill, but they annoy him."

"How's that possible?" The Kid said.

"Same way that damn sky is possible," Smith said. "Same way all of this is possible. Same way I'm back and different. Goddamn it, you have to trust me. We don't have time for explanation."

"I trust you," Payday said, slipped off her gun belt and punched out the ammunition with her thumb, took a bullet from Smith, and stuck it in one of the empty shell loops on her gun belt. The remaining loops filled with silver bullets.

"Damn," Cameahwait said.

"My thoughts exactly," The Kid said.

Each took a shell in turn. Smith said, "As long as you have one, you'll have plenty."

"And if you lose the last one?" Doc said.

"Then bend over and spread your ass and wait for the screwing by forces so big and bad they can't be imagined," Smith said.

"I'll be sure to hang onto one," Doc said. "So what's the plan?"

"I'm still sorting that out," Smith said.

PART FIVE:
The Plan

The best laid plans of mice and men often go awry.
INSPIRED BY THE ROBERT BURNS POEM, "TO A MOUSE."

⟨1⟩

The night was bright and the sky groaned. They all rode out of the cave, through the woods, and onto the trail, riding slowly along the tree-shadowed road.

"A moaning sky makes me nervous," said Double Shot, as he clopped along beside Smith.

"Sky make sound," Cameahwait said. "Not birds. No animals. Not good."

"He's right," Payday said. "The only thing you can hear is that noise in the heavens."

The moon wobbled. The sky creaked. The night shimmered and the stars wavered as they neared the town. The long shadows from the tree-lined road tumbled over them and seemed to have a life of their own, but there were still no sounds from birds and animals.

Double Shot said, "Now, I don't want to be someone who pisses in the soup, but I think you talked about a plan, and here we are, heading toward town, and if your plan is we ride in and whip his ass, I got to point out that hasn't worked so well in the past for us."

"What we need are reinforcements," Smith said.

"That would be nice," Double Shot said. "But in case you haven't noticed, we are short on reinforcements around here. You have us now, and we have you, and that pretty much ads up to everybody."

Smith stopped riding, dismounted. The others paused, slipped out of their saddles.

"If you're going to draw a line in the dirt," Double Shot said, "to indicate the town, the road, and you're going to show how we split up and come at it from all sides, I think that's not going to reassure me much."

"No," Smith said. "I said reinforcements, and I meant it."

"So no lines drawn in the dirt," Double Shot said.

"No," Smith said. "I'm going to deal cards."

"I like a good card game much as the next," The Kid said, "but that's it, we're going to stop for a little game of five card stud?"

"In a manner of speaking, yes," Smith said. "Maybe five card posse would be more accurate."

Smith reached into his coat pocket and pulled out the stack of cards. "I've been trying to avoid using these on account of who gave them to me. I figure help from him might have consequences."

"Him?" Payday said.

"Just who do you think I might be talking about?" Smith said.

"Are you trying to say God gave you these cards?" Doc said.

"Fella a little farther South," Smith said.

"The Devil?" The Kid said. "The Hell you say."

"Exactly," Smith said. "Everyone spread out a little, case this doesn't turn out quite the way I hope."

The group pulled at their horses and spread to opposite sides of the road. Smith stood in the center of the dirty track and looked up at the quivering moon. "This is our plan. Unless a certain Southern gentleman was fooling with me."

"Loco Weed," Cameahwait said.

"I hear that," said Double Shot. "And with a whisky chaser."

Smith held out the deck, took a deep breath, and dealt the first card. He dealt off the bottom. He thought that was appropriate. When he dealt, he let it go with a flick of the wrist. It coasted onto the road like a dry leaf. Everyone gathered around the card and looked at it. On it was a painting of a rough-looking woman with a face so ugly she could make birds fall from the sky. She wore a calico dress and a wide gun belt with a holstered pistol visible and a smaller Colt Navy stuck in the belt. She was astride a pinto pony, her dress bunched in the middle so that she could swing her legs into the stirrups. She had eyes like piss holes in the sand.

"So," The Kid said. "What we do is we watch you deal cards off the bottom—I noticed that—and toss them in the dirt. And let me tell you, if that's the Queen of your deck, you have one ugly set of cards there."

And then the card quivered.

The colors on the card beaded and boiled and ran together and made blended rivers of colors, and then a hot wind blew through carrying the stench of carrion. The wind wiggled the card, and the color rose up from it, rose up and stood up, and what replaced those rivers of color was a flesh and blood version of the woman on the card astride that pinto pony.

"Belle Star at your service," she said. "You might say a fella sent me."

"Belle Star," The Kid said. "But…"

"Yeah. I know," she said. "Not quite the looker the Dime Novels played me out to be. But I've had it rough, sonny. But you want to find out later if I can teach you how to really buck the tiger, I'm your lady."

"I'll pass on that," The Kid said.

"Maybe your balls haven't dropped yet," she said. "You have that look."

"They're just fine," The Kid said.

"One member of the posse," Smith said, and he flicked another card off the bottom onto the dusty road. "Now two."

The card sailed out and edged into the dirt and lay flat. The face of the card had a painting of a bearded man wearing a Confederate uniform that had seen better days. It was patched in places with colored cloth. The man had bandoleers crossing his chest. The bullets in them were shiny silver. He was astride a huge, palomino horse. He was slightly turned in the saddle, and revolvers could be seen in holsters on his hips, and there was another in his belt.

The paint ran together as before, and as before, it rose up and spread and formed the shape on the card, and then a hot air from nowhere whistled along the road and the paint became solid, alive and breathing.

The man looked at Smith and smiled. He was missing a tooth on the right side of his mouth.

"Hell, boy," the man said looking at Smith. "I know you. Between us I figured we killed a regiment."

Smith nodded. "Lady and gents. Bloody Bill Anderson."

"I want you to know I didn't volunteer to be here, as I heard you had you a change of heart about things, and you ain't the child-shooting, woman-killing bastard I once knew.",

"You're here because I called you here with the power of that card and the fellow who gave it to me. I'm giving the orders this time, Bill."

Bill sat silent, his hands on the pommel of his saddle. "Hell, it's all killing. All good."

Another card, and this time there was a man on the card and he was sitting on a sleek, black horse. A handsome man with a trim beard dressed all in black, including his hat. He had pale skin, blue eyes, and a short, red feather in his hat. The paint rose up and the hot wind came through and the man sitting there looked out at Smith and smiled. "Smith, you ole bastard. Done gone in cahoots with the denizens of fiery hell. You and me, and this fellow Bill, and I'm going to guess that lady there with the hatchet face—"

"Hey," Belle said. "There's some damn right ugly men too, you know."

"Yeah," said the man, "but I ain't one of them."

"Jesse," Smith said. "It's not really good to see you. But I'm glad you're here."

"Following orders. Though I don't want to."

"Wait," The Kid said. "Jesse? Jesse James?"

"One and the same," Smith said. "Got the back of his head blown off not that long ago. Everyone on these cards is dead. Sort of."

"How you hanging, Smith?" Jesse said.

"Low and to the left," Smith said.

"You know Frank surrendered?"

"I heard."

"I'd never have figured that."

"In one way or another," Smith said, "we all surrender."

Smith flicked another card. The card floated down to the dust. Everyone stared. On a great white horse, wearing a gray Confederate jacket, and black pants stuffed in tall black boots, a worn-out, white hat drooping over his head, was a bearded man. He had a face that made Belle Starr beautiful. His skin looked to have been soaked in sweat and dried out and creased with a hot branding iron. He wore five pistols. Two in holsters, two in his belt, and a .36 Navy Colt in an underarm holster. The same process came about, wiggling colors, a hot wind and rising colors, and then a man was sitting a horse.

"Quantrail," Smith said.

"I hate you," Quantrail said.

"You hate everyone, way I remember," Smith said.

"I liked my old daddy all right, the son-of-a-bitch, but you I hate. Goddamn traitor. Can't even go to hell and stay there. You got to buck and come back as someone who's trying to be worth a shit."

Payday said, "You know, I just thought I'd seen everything."

Smith flipped the last card.

And on the card was a big man on a big, chestnut horse. The big man wore a low-crowned, wide-brimmed, white hat. He had a mustache and shoulder-length blonde hair. He had a rugged handsomeness about him. Still, it was clearly a face that had seen plenty and not liked a lot of it, but that face hadn't lost its humor. He was leaning slightly forward on his horse. He wore a wide, red sash and two pearl-handled pistols stuck in it with the handles turned for cross draw action. He wore a yellow, fringed, leather jacked over a bright, red shirt, and his pants were dark leather and fringed as well. His boots were knee-high moccasins that matched his jacket.

"My god," Payday said. "I know who that is?"

"Who wouldn't?" Doubleshot said. "We've all seen the photographs, read all the Dime Novels."

"Wild Bill Hickok," Jimmy said.

"At your service," Wild Bill said. "And I say that with a bit of salt on my tongue. All you Johnny Rebs, and me a Union man. But I remember you, Smith. I remember you. You look the same… But different. I bet if I hadn't been in hell I wouldn't even recognize you. Gives you a kind of way of knowing your own. Or what used to be your own. I reckon you made some kind of deal with the Old Boy."

"Today I am no longer a Confederate, and I'm not Union either," Smith said. "We are all one thing and one thing only. We're a team. And these folks with me, they're part of that team. And you are by order of that smoky-hot bastard down below, at my service. You will remember that."

"Long as we get to kill something," Quantrail said. "I figure, like me, we all got the silver bullets."

"I'm all for that killing business too," Bloody Bill said.

"You will get to kill things that are already dead," Smith said. "And even for you Quantrail, that's going to be a first."

Cameahwait grunted, said, "Never heard of them. Should have sent Crazy Horse. Him I heard of."

"Crazy Horse didn't go to hell," Wild Bill said.

(2)

The moonlight lit the road up and there was a steady wind blowing in from the South. It carried that carrion stench with it. It was warm enough to draw sweat to the brow, even on a moonlit night. As they rode along, shapes sensed but not seen, shifted and rattled on dry leaves amongst the trees. A crow cawed in the depths of the woods, and in the distance there was a long drawn out howling made by wolves in concert.

Smith and Double Shot were in the lead, their familiar group and the new posse riding not far behind. Their horses' hooves made a clatter that seemed much too loud for comfort.

Smith glanced toward the forest on his left, then his right.

Double Shot did the same, said, "It seems odder than usual, and that's saying something."

"Beast not silent now," Cameahwait said.

"Signs and portents," Smith said. "Thing are realigning, and not for the better. Also, I think my boss is about, keeping an eye on things."

"If this boss is such a power, why isn't he doing this?" Double Shot said.

"The netherworld has rules it seems," Smith said. "And part of it is that overt acts of power done by the man himself are considered vulgar. And it may be that he has to have others do some of his biding. Again, netherworld rules. I have to obey them because he has to."

Double Shot turned on his horse and looked back at the posse hoofing along not far behind them. He said to Smith, "They're damn near as bad as who we're going after."

"I figured the Lady's Temperance Movement was the wrong kind of posse for the job. Still, I hesitated to bring them along at all. But, it's come to that. And they may not be enough. But the way things are we're going to have to do something even if it's wrong."

Double Shot nodded. "Reckon so."

"One thing though. Hickok. He's all right. I'm not even sure why he went to the far, hot south unless it was for something he done we don't know anything about. As honorable and as true a shot never existed. I know all these folks a little, except Belle. I've just heard of her."

"Any of it what you heard about her good?"

"Nope."

Payday and the others began to catch up with Smith and Double Shot. Pretty soon they were all together in a tight line of horses.

"One cannon shot and our posse is over," said Double Shot.

"Got to hope they don't have a cannon," Hickok said.

"The tower is where the bad stuff is happening," Smith said. "That's all we really need to know. Quill will end up there. If not now, later. If we can get him before he gets there, all the better. After he gets there, we don't have much time to do what needs to be done."

Hickok laughed. "Then we'll have to take less time, won't we?"

"Exactly," Smith said.

Hickok edged his horse closer to Smith.

"Do you remember that time in Dodge when you and me—"

"Another time," Smith said, "and another me. Or so I like to think."

"I figure that's right," Hickok said. "We was all different then."

"But Hell for you, Bill? I don't get it. Even that time in Dodge, I was the one started that mess. You just finished it because you had to."

"Limbo. The waiting room Snappy calls it. I wasn't all bad, and I wasn't all good."

"Who is?"

"Well, some of us, like me, straddle the fence a little too much. You were definitely on the dark side of the fence, but you've been given another shot. Good for you. Don't blow it."

Smith glanced at Payday. She pretended to look off and not pay attention.

"Nothing you ever did matched me at my worst," Smith said to Hickok. "Nothing."

"I'll take you at your word," Hickok said. "Hoss. Here's something else. We aren't exactly sneaking. I mean, we all know why we're here and what we're supposed to do. We got some thin instructions from the boss, that if you called we were to come, but these bad folks, they'll know we're coming."

"Of course they will," Smith said. "But we don't have time for sneaking. Time is nearly up. It's assholes and elbows, and the time to do something is now. That's why I have you five added to the crew. It has to be straight-forward and done with a flair, like a tornado throwing bullets."

"Point taken," Hickok said.

Smith boosted himself ahead of the others, wheeled his horse. His friends and the new-found posse slowed and gathered their mounts around him. Smith and Payday exchanged a long glance.

Smith said, "All right. We've come to it. The tower is where the bad stuff happens. It's going to happen soon. We're going to meet some hard business and pretty quick. The tower is where Quill will end up. If we can get to him before he gets there, all the better. If he gets to the tower, well, he has to be stopped before he can do what he wants to do, because if he does, the world shifts, and if you think it's a shit hole now, it'll seem like a bed of roses after that. The piece of moon on either side of the tower, the center of that, that's the bell tower, if you need that explained to you. It's where the big church bell hangs. That's the gate for The Old Ones. Now, I wouldn't know an Old One from a retired watchmaker, but I do know this. They ain't good folks. In fact, they ain't exactly folks. I can't tell you what will happen if they come through, other than to say it will be bad beyond measure or imagination. What I'm supposed to do when I get to the bell tower I have yet to figure. It's kind of learn as you go, but I figure if The Bartender wanted me to do, I must be the man for the job, least as he sees it."

The others mumbled about for a few moments. All except Cameahwait. He grunted once. He might have been concerned or just passing a fart. With him it was hard to tell.

"So," Bloody Bill said. "We didn't 'spect we was called here to take a pony ride around a veranda somewheres. We even got some idea what we're up against, thanks to the old boy down there, but whatever it is, jaw-ing ain't going to solve it. Let's go kill something, even if it's re-kill."

"Killing is our business," Jesse said.

"Remember. I give the orders," Smith said. "When there are orders to give. Most of us here are stone cold killers. We've had practice. So I won't need to give many orders, but if I give one, I expect it to be obeyed."

"Good enough," Will Bill said.

"First order is simple," Smith said. "Follow me."

The trail widened and the woods faded away and seemed to flee across a clearing into blue-black shadow. The clearing had formerly been farm land. The crops had grown tall and green, but now the crops were gone, tall grass had replaced them, and the grass had died and turned crisp and dry as an old, corn tortilla.

Ahead of them, in the distance, they could see the town and they could see the bell tower. It rose up high in the night and was bright by moonlight, and the moon was split from full view on either side of it; it hung in place and was no longer rising.

They began to ride faster, and then, Hickok, who was riding near Smith said, "We been seen, Hoss."

"Assholes on both sides," Cameahwait called out from the back.

"He ain't really a talker," Smith said to Hickok. "But when he does, it's usually about something."

The riders came out of the woods on their bony mounts, and the warm air turned warmer, as if with their arrival came summer. Then, just as inexplicably, the air turned chill like the first sure day of solid winter. The world and all its structure were coming undone.

"Thing is," Smith said. "I got to make that tower. Everything else is just a fly in the ointment."

Smith broke his horse into a faster run, heading straight toward the tower. There was no way they were going to make it before the dead riders caught up with them, but if he could break free.

Double Shot yelled, "Smith. You and Payday. Go for it. We'll stop these son-of-a-bitches."

Smith waved his hand above his head in thanks, urged Shadow forward. The great horse seemed more to leap than to gallop, covering vast expanses of ground. Payday came behind him, not too far away, but enough to become a kind of rear guard. She yipped and yelled and whirled her whip above her head.

(3)

The dead galloped in from both sides, pressing down on the ragged posse. The posse rode hard and straight, staying to the center of Main Street. Guns were fired by the dead folks, and then gunfire was returned. For a moment no one on either side was hit.

Hickok yelled. "Protect Smith at all costs."

Smith looked back and saw the posse had started to fire at the dead riders. They were letting him and Payday break free of the pack, giving them distance, though some of the dead riders had broken ranks and were coming after them.

Payday rose up in her stirrups and swung her whip above her head as gunfire roared and bullets buzzed around her. Her whip cracked, and it was sure, snapping the tops of rotten heads, breaking them open, tumbling dead riders from their horses and smacking them on the ground. She even snapped it hard enough to crack horse heads and bring them down, skidding in the dirt, skidding into sliding meat and finally into puffs of dust.

Behind them posse bullets whizzed. Dead heads exploded with brains and blood that had long dried to a powder fine as sand. But something in their dead skulls made them walk, and think, to the degree they were able to think, and the blasts to their heads brought them down.

Cameahwait strung arrows as he rode. He pulled them from his quiver and to his bow with swift precision. They took flight as rapidly as you might cock a Winchester and fire it, always striking their marks, driving arrows through dead riders' heads.

Smith and Payday were well ahead now, riding hard as they could go for the tower. Behind them the street was stirred with dust from ghouls and the posse. The dusty cloud spun and darkened. Then there was the sound of snorting horses and coughing men, gunfire and yells. The dust gathered so thick little could be seen.

Except for Smith and Payday, they had all come together in the middle of the street in a kind of dusty tornado. Then the wind, sometimes hot, sometimes cold, moved the dust, and when it moved there was a brief vision of what might have been a mural on the wall of Snappy's bar; a tableau in and of Hell. Warriors dead and alive in close struggle, a few guns firing, but mostly hand to hand fighting from the backs of horses, rifles swinging, fists flying. Cameahwait in close with his hard and solid bow, using it like a club. Belle Star leaning out from her horse with blackened teeth barred, stabbing at dead heads with a bowie knife near big as a Centurion's sword. Jesse James cracking heads with his pistol, Hickok with a revolver in either hand, doing the same, showing off ambidextrous skills that would have put an octopus to shame.

Then the dust cloud swirled again and gathered around the riders, and they were lost to view, the only knowledge of them the clanking of metal, the snorting of horses, the grunts of riders on both sides. The dust grew so thick that finally the sounds stopped, as neither side knew friend from foe, and then along came that wind, hot this time, and the dust spread apart like a gauzy curtain and dropped to the ground.

And there, as if frozen, once again was revealed that tableau from the depths of hell, the dead riders and the posse, but not moving now. All of the posse were still mounted, but on the ground were many finished ghouls, lying in twisted heaps, their heads burst open and leaking, dead horses. Rotting arms and legs were spread about among hats and weapons and dead ghoul horses, and then the bodies turned to a soft, powdered dust, and the wind picked it up and away it went.

The living and the living dead sat their horses and stared at one another, no one moving, and then Belle Star smiled her ruined-tooth smile, and yelled a yell that came from way down deep, from the bowels of her recent hellish home, and everything she had ever done that had got her to that hot place, rose up and out of her in that noise.

Things came unstuck. The horses moved, the dust swirled again, and once more the ball was rolling. Jesse James took a shot in the arm and fell from his horse. On the ground he rolled to his feet, bleeding, grabbed a dropped rifle and started backing down the street, firing the weapon as fast as he could cock it with his injured arm. It wasn't fast enough. The back of the alley was now plugged with ghouls. Jesse spun this way and that, trying to bring down as many as he could, with hope to open a path. But the Winchester clicked empty. Jesse dropped the rifle, pulled a scabbard knife from the back of his belt. They descended on him. He stuck one dead cowboy in the head and re-killed it before they covered him with snapping teeth and he went down in a gush of blood and screams of pain. When the horde of ghouls rose up from the body, what was left of Jesse was a skull dangling flesh, a rib cage, and a wide pool of blood sinking into the dirty street. One ghoul, a young woman in a stained yellow dress, was on her knees lapping at the blood like a hound lapping water.

The posse was separated now, and Belle Starr was screaming happily at the top of her lungs, blasting away with her revolver. Her horse stumbled, and down it and Belle went. The horse found its feet, bolted free, too fast for her to catch it.

Belle scrambled to her feet, found herself on the edge of the street with a building near her back. She backed toward it, reloading as she went, bullets flying all around her. When her back touched the wall, she was still filling the cylinders with ammunition. Bullets took off her black hat, pierced the edges of her dress, pinching flesh, but failed to bite deep. Splinters flew from the wall.

Double Shot rode out of a wad of dust like a jinn from a bottle, rode straight for Belle; blasting away as he went, popping dead folk with every shot. And then his gun was empty and he was against the wall next to Belle.

Ghouls dismounted, started walking toward them, handguns and rifles at the ready.

"One damn time in my life I done something truly brave," Double Shot said, "and it ain't working out."

"Regretting it," Belle said.

"A little."

Double Shot pulled the last silver bullet from his belt. The belt refilled when he did. He loading fast as he could, but it was not fast enough. The ghouls' bullets were striking them this time, making their bodies dance against the wall, blood spewing and misting, orange in the moonlight, splattering against the wall, soaking into the wood, splashing in the street. Down went Double Shot, and down went Belle, leaking and not moving.

The dead folk swooped down on them like vultures, ripping off arms and legs, biting into flesh, feasting as if it was the last buffet on earth and only two bits a wagon load.

Smith and Payday saw ahead of them a street full of ghouls. Some on horseback, most on foot, coming along the center of the street and down the boardwalks on either side. Some had rakes and hoes and sticks and rocks, a few had pistols, rifles and knives.

"We got to make the tower," Smith said. "But we can't ride through that."

"You have to make the tower," Payday said. She spurred her horse forward and the whip whirled above her head, sang through the air and popped an eye from a ghoul's head. Another snap of the whip and she wrapped it around another ghoul's head. With a flick of her wrist the rotten noggin came off, spun about and smashed into a support post on the board walk.

The whip flashed again, swirled around a porch support. Payday danced her horse backwards, the post cracked, gave, brought the roof tumbling down on the heads of those beneath it. Legs and arms thrashed out from under the wreckage like spider legs under a boot heel.

Smith didn't abandon her.

"I'm not going without you," he called out across the throng of dead folk.

"Well damn you," Payday said. "There's only the world at stake, and it's the only one we got."

Payday recoiled her whip, looped it over her shoulder, swung beneath her horse as she pulled her pistols again and rode hanging by one boot heel clamped to the saddle horn, both hands firing revolvers. She charged past Smith before he realized what was happening.

Out of an alley came a little girl with a shovel. Her little teeth were barred. Smith shot her right in those little teeth, knocking them out, taking away the back of her head, sending skull fragments skittering down the alley.

Smith put his heels to Shadow and the great horse plunged right through the opening Payday was creating. The dead tried to close on them, but the move had been so quick and so startling, by the time they had collected their dull wits, Payday and her mount, Smith and Shadow, had dashed through the gap.

As he rode through, Smith looked back. The ghouls were filling in behind him, and beyond that, back behind them, Smith could see Wild Bill whirling his horse in a circle, the reins in his teeth, firing as he did, a pistol in either hand. It looked like some kind of circus trick, except every time his six-guns snapped, dead folks lost the caps of their skulls.

Once Smith and Payday reached a rise in the street, Smith turned to look, saw Hickok once more, no longer spinning, but riding right at the mass of regrouping dead, drawing their attention from Smith and Payday.

Hickok returned his revolvers to his sash, pulled his rifle from its saddle boot, cocked it and snapped off shots one handed, trying to push through the rotten throng of hungry corpses to create a rear guard.

One of the dead folk grabbed at Hickok's boot, latched on, and pulled. Hickok kicked his boot free. As he did, the ghoul bit through the boot as if it was soft licorice, ending up with nothing than leather and air in its mouth. Hickok slung the rifle out with one hand and smashed the dead thing's brain, dropping it and the boot it was holding.

The dead closed about Hickok's horse, biting it, pulling at it, grabbing at Hickok. Hickok and the horse went down.

His bravery had given Smith and Payday time to near the top of the hill. Smith paused, took a stick of dynamite from his saddle bags, lit it, and as a horde of dead rose up the hill, he tossed it.

The explosion nearly rocked Smith and Payday off their horses. Bodies of the dead scattered in all directions, sprinkles of dead flesh and dried blood splattered against Smith's face. When the smoke and dust cleared there was a heap of dead folks, splattered about like shit in a cow lot.

"That gives us a bit of space," Smith said.

Not far from where they sat on their horses was the bell tower.

Hickok had somehow survived without being bit. His clothes had been gnawed, jaws had snapped on the brim of his hat, jerking it from his head, but he had swung his pistols and fired them, and kicked and shoved, and had broken free, limping along, wearing one boot. The dead filed after him. Hickok broke for the boardwalk, kicked at the door on the Post Office, and it sprang open. He darted inside, but the dead still came.

The Kid fired his revolvers and ghouls went down, but then they had his horse, tugging at it, pulling at the belly band, the bridle, the stirrups. The horse fell and so did The Kid. The Kid broke free, snapping his gun barrels against the heads of ghouls, kicking them back, swinging elbows, and then to his surprise ghouls nearby started falling around him. They had arrows through their heads. Even in the bright moonlight he had not seen them at first, and had only heard them in the manner of a swift wind passing.

Cameahwait.

The Kid didn't have time to locate him. There was a clearing that had been made by his swinging pistols and Cameahwait's swift arrows, and it was his only route, and he took it.

It wasn't much of a clearing, but there was running room, and he ran, found an alleyway. The Kid beat feet down that alleyway, and behind him flowed a running, hooting horde of dead folk.

Some of the dead looked up and saw him.

Cameahwait.

He was on the rooftops.

There was nothing the ghouls could do. He was a momentary silhouette and then he was moving. Cameahwait had long lost his horse, and silent as a dream, he had taken to the tops of the buildings and was running along them, making what might be thought of as impossible leaps from one roof to another, sometimes stringing his bow at a run, firing arrows into the midst of the dead folk, making one incredible shot in mid-leap, putting the arrow through a ghoul's eye.

Finally, his quiver nearly empty, vaulting from one rooftop to another, he ran to the back of a building and disappeared from view.

Quantrail and Bloody Bill rode their horses into the hordes, reins in their teeth, their hands filled with blazing revolvers. The horde swelled. It was as if they were growing up from the ground. Soon the Rebel warriors were surrounded. They emptied their pistols. Dead folk and dead horses heaped about them. And then a great moan rose up from the dead. A great moan of hunger and anger and determination, and then the dead were on them, grabbing at their horses, pulling them over, pulling them down into their midst.

Up through the huddle of dead rose Bloody Bill, cursing and swinging the barrels of his revolvers as clubs. Teeth snapped from behind him, buried in his shoulder, and then down he went, but then he was up again, shaking the dead off of him like a dog shakes water. Bloody Bill fought his way free, ran to the side of a building with a trellis for flowers, now nothing more than brown, twisted vines, and up the trellis he went, like a monkey. At the roof of the building he collapsed, lay on his back, bleeding from the bite. He reloaded his revolver with the silver bullets from Hell.

Quantrail, lying against the body of his horse, his leg being chewed on by children, screamed in pain and shoved his gun barrel under his chin, pulled the trigger. The revolver's cylinder rolled on an empty.

Quantrail laughed, and then they had him, were all over him like a skin rash.

In a moment, there was nothing left of Quantrail but some gnawed clothes and some shiny buttons. The ghouls stood up, bellies swollen. Some of what had been Quantrail oozed out of belly holes in the rottenest of the dead.

There was a shadow that spread wide, and then there was a sound of wings beating. Against the moonlight flew Quill, dark and hawkish. He was descending on Bloody Bill who was up on the roof of the bank, wounded, thinking he was bound to turn to one of them soon. By this time he had reloaded his revolver, and he made himself stand. It was all he could do to stand. He wobbled. He heard the screech of Quill high up in the sky, lifted his face toward the sound, and down came Quill. A flash of shadow, a beat of wings, extended talons. Bloody Bill howled his rebel yell and lifted his pistol and started snapping off shots. They hit Quill, and the silver made him screech, but still he came, like an avalanche, snatching Bloody Bill's head as if it were a melon, squeezing, squirting goo in all directions, and then Quill rose up, way up, carrying Bloody Bill's dead and dangling body by its crushed skull. Higher went Quill, up into the moonlight, over the woods. Then higher yet, climbing up into the golden-lit sky until he was a dark dot with Bloody Bill in his talons, dangling like a mouse. And then Quill dropped Bloody Bill. The body fell straight and fast into the woods, where it struck with a splat, striking so hard Bloody Bill's ribcage poked up through his body. That was all for Bloody Bill.

A raccoon peeked out from behind a tree trunk, realizing he had just been delivered a hot lunch.

Even as Smith and Payday rode up the hill toward the bell tower, no longer aware of what was going on behind them, the moon, split by the tower, grew big and fat like a golden tick gorged on blood. It wobbled.

It was starting, Smith thought. They were running late. The moon was about to activate the spell, and when it did the world was nothing more than a bug to be stepped on by The Old Ones.

⟨4⟩

Smith and Payday were two lone riders in the swollen moonlight, on an empty stretch of dusty street, and then they were two riders in a swarming midst of dead folk arriving on foot. From between the buildings they came, rotten ones straight from the graveyard, a few still with a touch of primrose about their cheeks. They were like a typhoon of rotting, dripping flesh, their teeth snapping like animal traps. They rolled their putrid tide toward Smith and Payday, who fired their weapons, dropping many, but not driving them back. They came from alleys and leaked out of buildings into the street, scuttling over one another in their passion to reach Smith and Payday, who by this time had pulled their horses side by side and stopped. They had to stop. There was nowhere to go.

"Looks like the jig is up," Payday said. "Shoot me, save one for yourself, Smith."

"Not likely," Smith said.

At that moment there was a screech. Smith turned in his saddle, Payday in hers. They saw Quill then. He came down from on high like an arrow, shooting toward them.

"If things weren't bad enough," Smith said. And then he pulled the reins on Shadow. Shadow bolted forward, and as he went, Smith reached out and slapped Payday's horse's haunch, and it too leaped forward, riding them straight into a pack of ghouls who went whirling before Shadow as if hit by a locomotive. Payday rode hard, leaning low. She saw the great shadow of Quill running along the ground beside her, and the shadow swelled. Payday, feeling the hot breath of Quill on her neck, swung to the side of her horse and twisted in such a way that she could fire a shot upwards. The silver bullet hit Quill and he squealed, but it didn't stop him, merely startled him. Down he came, grabbing the horse's head and lifting the animal up. Payday went tumbling into the street. The ghouls surrounded her.

Smith turned on Shadow, slipping his feet from the stirrups, sliding until he was sitting backwards in the saddle, the way he had done in his rebel days to sometimes deal with pursuers, the same way he had seen Payday do. He started firing his revolvers, filling Quill full of silver. The silver wounds hissed and spat white smoke. Quill dropped the horse into a broken wad of bones and flesh into the street, and then flapped upwards into the night sky.

The ghouls were closing on Payday. Her revolvers were empty. She holstered them and turned to her whip, cracking heads with snaps of her wrist. In that moment Smith thought she was like a goddess of war come down from that gold moon to drive back the devilish hordes with nothing more than a magic whip and will power. Except she wasn't magic. She was flesh and blood, and exactly what the hungry dead wanted. Fresh meat.

Smith, had holstered his revolvers, and now he had his rifle, and the rifle cracked time and again. The ghouls that were closing on Payday began to drop like rotten fruit. Smith stuck the rifle back in the saddle sheath, rode fast toward Payday, and as the dead surrounded them, he reached and took Payday's hand and swung her on the back of Shadow. The horse reared. Hooves flashed. Heads were cracked and other ghouls were driven back. Smith bolted Shadow through the mass of dead like a bullet through wind, knocking the teeth-snapping, clutching monsters in all directions. The ghouls turned then on Payday's dead horse, an easier meal.

The ghouls ripped at its belly with teeth and hands and knives, ripped and pulled long lines of steaming guts from its wounds, chewed and smacked over the remains.

It was the break they needed.

But then, a sound. The fluttering of wings

Smith glanced up.

Quill was diving for them. Smith jerked his rope off the saddle horn, whipped it above his head. As Quill swooped down and tried to grab Payday off the back of the horse, and as Payday took evasive action by leaning way out and onto the side of Shadow, Smith's rope uncoiled, sailed through the air and looped over Quill's head. Smith wrapped the rope around the saddle horn, way he would if he had roped a calf. He put his boot heels to Shadow, and the great horse leaped. It was such a jump for a moment the animal seemed like Pegasus taking flight. Quill was yanked down to the ground, where he hit the street in dusty hops.

That's when Smith saw a possibility.

The door of the Assay Office.

Under the overhang Smith went, ducking his head so as not to lose it to a rafter. Payday swung back up behind Smith, pressed her head into Smith's back. Shadow hit the door with his chest. It flew open and slammed against the wall. In they rode, dragging Quill behind him. Quill's wings spread and caught the doorway, but still Smith rode, urging Shadow up a flight of rickety stairs. Up and up, pulling until the door frame began to give way. Quill was making more noise than a bird sanctuary. Quill's talons flashed out and the rope was snapped free. Quill fluttered backwards and into the street, then with an angry yell, took to the sky.

Smith wheeled Shadow on the tight stair landing, a move no ordinary mount could manage, but Shadow did it with ease. Down the stairs they rode, Smith pulling his rifle from its sheath, Payday her revolvers. At the bottom of the stairs Smith leaped off Shadow, ran to the window, knocking out glass with the barrel of the rifle. Payday squatted down to reload her pistols.

Outside things had gone from bad to worse.

The moon was sweeping down low as if on a string, falling into position more securely behind the tower, the light of it shining through the gap in the structure. The air became cold as an old Blue Norther.

Their sight of the bell tower was at an angle, but Smith and Payday could see it quite clearly as the street turned slight and gave them view.

"Damn," he said. "We have to get to the tower."

"Nice idea, but not likely," Payday said, looking out at the gathering crowd of dead folk. With her revolvers loaded, she holstered them, stood up and pushed the door shut, dragged a chair over and placed it under the latch. "That ought to hold them long enough for us to say 'Oh hell'."

"If that long," Smith said. "We either get eaten, or The Old Ones get loose. Either way we lose."

And then they saw Cameahwait. He came running along the tops of buildings, leaping from one to the other, the last of his arrows flying, whipping through the heads of the ghouls, dropping them, and then, as if he had been nothing more than a swirl of leaves, he was gone.

"Well, someone besides us is still alive. And now he's gone."

But he wasn't.

He came out of the shadows on the roof, became whole in the moonlight, hit the ground light as a bird landing, charged straight into a pack of ghouls, swinging his heavy bow, knocking the dead right and left. Teeth snapped in the moonlight, hands grasped, legs even tried to trip, but Cameahwait leapt and dodged and leaped and rolled, and pretty soon he was approaching the Assay Office.

"Open the door," Smith yelled. "I'll cover him."

Cameahwait came running and the ghouls came running, almost grabbing him, but Smith's pistols barked, and down they went, heads splintered. Then Payday had the door open. Cameahwait shot through the doorway, did a tumbling roll, came up on his feet, his bow clutched close to his chest.

"Howdy," he said.

Payday slammed the door, but the dead were there, shoving at it. She and Cameahwait managed to shove it closed and hook the chair beneath the latch again. Now the ghouls came to the burst window, began reaching through, trying to grab Smith. He backed up, revolvers firing, the dead dropping.

Payday grabbed Shadow's reins and began leading him up the stairs, Cameahwait with her, Smith pulled up the rear, backing up the stairs blasting away.

Cameahwait said something in his native language that even without benefit of translation was obviously of a negative nature.

The chair against the door strained and snapped. The dead came in through the open doorway and the broken window, and then there was the sound of other windows breaking, and the room below filled with ghouls.

(5)

The Kid outran the dead for awhile. Went out of a store, through an alley, and the ghouls ran behind him like children playing chase. But The Kid was fast, and he was clever. He wove in and out of buildings and finally came back to the store where the chase had started, having lost his pursuers, at least for a moment. He was in what remained of the dress shop Smith had blasted. The front of it was a shambles, but there was still a frame and roof, and there were all manner of dresses and bolts of cloth, odds and ends, broken shelves and overturned counters lying about. The Kid could hear his heart beating. He was shaking and he was covered in blood. None of it his.

He went behind a counter and sat there with his back against it, took a breather. He checked his pistols. Partially loaded. He took the time to reload them with silver bullets, and then he took a deep breath. Have to move on, he told himself. Got to help Smith get to that tower.

And then he asked himself, what if Smith was no longer alive? What then?

Maybe he could get to the tower himself. But if he did, he had no idea what he was supposed to do to stop the entrance of The Old Ones. All he could do was hope for the best, and if it was his to figure in the end, he'd have to do some damn good figuring.

The Kid moved out from behind the counter and went softly to the back door, eased it open, and standing right there not two feet away, so close he could smell its foul, dead breath, was a ghoul with two shiny pistols in cross-draw holsters. He wore his hat pushed back and his nose had fallen off his face, one shoulder sagged abnormally under his shirt, as if the weight of the cloth was just too much. They were standing only a foot apart.

"Howdy there," the ghoul said, two teeth falling out of his mouth.

"Howdy, asshole," The Kid said.

The ghoul made as if to draw. The Kid reached out fast and drew the ghoul's pistols from his belt before the ghoul could lay hands on them, pointed them at him, spun them on his fingers, and replaced them in the ghoul's holsters.

The Kid said, "How's that for some shit?"

The ghoul looked impressed, smiled his gapped teeth. "That was pretty good."

The ghoul went for his pistols again, but The Kid was faster. He had them before the ghoul could touch them. He spun them again, cracked the ghoul over the head with both barrels, and returned the guns once again to the ghoul's holsters.

"That hurt," the ghoul said. The ghoul's rotting head was bent in at the top like a collapsing cake. "Least I think it did."

"This is going to be worse."

The Kid drew his revolvers, poked them in the ghoul's face, and fired, blasting the ghoul's head completely off its shoulders. The body stood for a moment. Smoke drifted up from the remains of the head, and then the dead man, affected by the silver, began to come apart, his legs turned to powder and leaked out his pants legs, and what was left of him collapsed on top of his boots in a pile of decay and shards of bone.

The Kid raced away toward the tower on foot. Out in the street, the sounds of struggle and gunfire had gone silent. The Kid had a feeling that wasn't good for his side. For all he knew, he was all that was left.

As he passed the corner of a building, he heard shots from the Assay Office. He looked across the street. The dead were flocking there. That meant inside there were living people. It stood to reason those people would be among those he had come with to town.

As the guns popped, he saw ghouls near the window start to come apart and dissolve into dust.

Yep. That would be part of his posse all right.

Wild Bill came out of hiding, found a horse.

It was saddled and frightened, but as it came running along the alley, he noted that it was one that had belonged to Belle Starr. The saddle had marks on it where fingernails had grabbed at it, but the horse seemed strong and uninjured, only frightened. Hickok grabbed at it, swung up on its back, just making it before the horse rode out from under him. The horse set out for the distant line of pines, bathed in moonlight in such a way it made them look like a mountain ridge.

Wild Bill turned the horse. It was a good horse and a good smooth turn. Wild Bill pulled it to a tight stop, reached out and rubbed its head.

"Easy, boy. We ain't through here yet."

The horse snorted, began to calm.

"Easy," Wild Bill said, and continued to rub its head. "Easy now. We got some things to do."

Wild Bill sat on the horse until it was calm. While he sat he reloaded his pistols, packed the cylinders with the silver bullets.

"Now, we done got ourselves ready, don't we?"

The horse snorted, but had relaxed considerably.

Wild Bill took the horse at a trot along the back way of the buildings. He could think of only one way they needed to go. Toward the tower, shiny with moonlight, high up on the hill; a beacon of finality.

And then he heard a chorus of gunfire.

"Yee-haw," The Kid said, and came charging across the road, running full out. Ghouls turned toward him, and when they did, The Kid, having had plenty of practice now, swung his revolvers, cracking heads, and then he was in the midst of them. Ghouls fired at him, missed, knocked holes in their own comrades, blew off parts and exploded heads.

The Kid saw the water trough ahead of him, leaped for it, hit one foot on its edge, sprang from there like a rabbit, landed with one foot on a horse rail, leaped onto the shoulder of a ghoul, rode him down, hit the boardwalk in front of the open window of the Assay office, balled up and rolled through, his boots flying up and knocking out the remains of the window glass. He rolled across the floor like a doodle bug, came to his feet. The room was filling with ghouls, but on the stairway he saw Smith, Cameahwait, and Payday, and on the landing above it, Smith's horse, standing there like some kind of mythical creature, looking down as if from Olympus. He fought his way to them. Smith came down the stairs and out on the floor, swinging his pistols, helping The Kid make it back to their last stand on the stairs.

And then came Wild Bill, riding his horse right up on the boardwalk, using the horse like a battering ram. Bill ducked under the doorway just in time not to lose his head, but the ghouls grabbed at the horse, and in an instant it was out from under him. Bill fought his way in, kicking and hammering and shooting toward the stairs where the others waited and were firing at the ghouls, helping his progress.

Wild Bill's heart filled with temporary hope.

The ghouls stank, their odor filled the room. It was wall to wall rot.

The Kid and Wild Bill were on the stairs now, and they were all firing at the ghouls, and the ghouls were firing back, but they were such bad shots their guns might as well have been empty. Most were without guns, having emptied their shells, and they were instead trying to mount the stairs with their pistols held as clubs.

Cameahwait looked at The Kid and Hickok, said, "About time."

Payday bolted upstairs, raced past Shadow, and into the room off the landing. A moment later she was out again, carrying two small, but heavy looking cloth bags. She dropped them on the landing, untied the string at the top of one. It fell open. Her hand dipped in, and when it lifted out, it was full of silver dust.

Of course. The Assay Office. It was where the silver was weighed and collected during mining times. It was exactly what the ghouls didn't like, and Payday had doped that out.

Payday tossed the silver at the ghouls at the bottom of the stairs. Wild Bill and Smith were reloading, and The Kid was in need of it. Cameahwait was out of arrows. He had finally broken his bow on a dead head, and had drawn his knife. He held it ready for action.

The dust Payday tossed sailed high and came down like silver rain. There was a scorching sound and screams from the ghouls as the silver bit into them. Flesh and bone collapsed beneath the dust, ran in wet, fleshy streams across the floor.

Wild Bill yelled out, "Way to go girl."

Now the defenders were loaded up and firing and emptying their weapons again, but even more effective was Payday with her handfuls of silver dust. She came down the stairs tossing it, and then across the floor tossing it. The ghouls were driven back and away from her. Out the door and back through the open windows they went, moving quickly when they could beat the flying dust, and dissolving when they couldn't, leaving only their ragged clothes behind and piles of boiling liquid that dried and powdered almost instantly. Even their footwear was not enough to insulate them from the dust on the floor. The silver ate through their boots and shoes, as if their dead flesh was too close to the dust and it was hungry for them. It dissolved them from the leather soles up.

Soon the room was empty of them, and they gathered on the boardwalk and in the street.

A cheer went up from the remains of the posse.

"Good thinking," Smith said.

"I know," Payday said, and she began spreading silver over the floor, flipping it out of the bag like she was tossing chicken feed. "They won't want to step on this. And the room up there, it's filled with bags of dust, and there are even chunks of ore lying about."

Smith raced up the stairs, tossed the other bag Payday had left on the stairs to Wild Bill, who grabbed it, jerked the tie loose, and started doing the same thing that Payday was doing, powdering the floor with silver dust. Smith disappeared briefly into the office where there was an open safe (probably left that way when the ghoul panic began), and inside it there were many small bags of silver. There was a scale on a table, and in the scale was a pile of silver dust. Huge chunks of ore were scattered about, knocked here and there during the panic.

Smith grabbed a couple bags of silver, raced out, tossed one down to The Kid, the other to Cameahwait. He went back and got one for himself, and then, leaving Shadow on the landing, he carried the remaining bag with him.

At the bottom they worked together to cover the floor in an even layer of silver dust, especially around windows and doorways. Already there were shoving sounds at the back door, but as Smith tossed the dust against it, and a bit of it went up and under the crack beneath the door, the pounding stopped abruptly and was replaced by the sound of fast scuttling.

"Good God," Smith said. "This has been here all the time. It might have been good to know."

"We should have realized it," Payday said. "That's what kept this town alive. Silver mines."

They were gathered on the stairs now, making sure their weapons were fully loaded.

"Well," Wild Bill said. "I been to a dozen county fairs, married a lady that worked in the circus, and watched a man fuck a goat in Illinois once. It was a dare. But this day has been an original."

"Nothing else," The Kid said, "that ought to hold them damn eaters for awhile."

"But we're held as well," Smith said. "And we got a job to do."

Smith jumped to his feet and started up the stairs. The others followed, Cameahwait leading Shadow inside.

In the Assay office there was a large window without glass that opened with two wide shutters. Smith threw them open. From there was a clear view of the tower and the bell, the big gold moon behind the tower. The moon throbbed like a blister. The light from it vibrated as if the moon were a pond into which a large stone had been cast.

The others gathered around Smith, checked out the tower and the moon and all its unusual light.

"Kind of pretty," Payday said.

"How pretty depends on how much you'll enjoy The Old Ones and the end of the world," Smith said.

"Pretty sure it won't be that much," Payday said.

Cameahwait grunted.

(6)

"If you can get to the tower, you know what to do, I reckon," Wild Bill said. "Or so I've been assuming. All I know is the card called me up and the basic information was given to me, as it was given to the others, by Snappy beforehand. But what to do when we get to the tower, that's your assignment, Smith."

"Well, if we don't stop The Old Ones from coming through, Hell is going to start looking like a vacation spot," Smith said. "Then again, not even it will exist."

"The bell tower is close, and yet, so far away," Payday said.

There was a double barrel shotgun mounted on the wall. Cameahwait took it down, blew off the dust near the hammers, cracked it open. It was loaded. He pinched out the loads.

"I like shotgun," Cameahwait said.

"Thought you were a bow and arrow guy?" The Kid said.

"Like knife, club, bow and arrow, shotgun. Cannon if have one. Like shotgun, though."

Cameahwait placed the shotgun on the table, next to the scale, and began peeling back the ends of the shotgun loads. He scooped silver dust from the scale on the table with the scoop, poured some on top of the loads of metal shot. He pinched the open ends of the paper loads tight, reloaded the shotgun with them. He found more shotgun shells in a drawer, and outfitted them the same way while his comrades watched. In the drawer Smith saw there were chunks of silver ore. In fact, he was really noting now how many large chunks of silver were scattered about the room. He had noticed before, but hadn't realized just how much there was. There were all manner of silver ornaments as well, including wall trim. All of it in tribute to what made Falling Rock famous, and the only thing that had made anyone want to come there in the first place.

"Nice," said The Kid, as Cameahwait finished up putting silver dust in the shotgun shells.

"Works for me," Wild Bill said. "Hey... What's that?"

Then heard thumping sounds. Loud hammering. Rapid sawing. Then many hammers and saws. It went on for some time. Leaving Shadow in the office, they went downstairs and looked out the busted window, into the glow of the hot moonlight.

At first it looked as if the ghouls had abandoned town, except for the rapid pounding and sawing sounds coming from the livery. Smith thought to take advantage of the absence of the ghouls, jump on Shadow and ride to the bell tower to do what he had to do. Which he still had to figure out.

But before he could think on that for very long, there was movement. Out into that unnaturally warm moonlight the ghouls filed out of the livery. A number of them were walking tall and high on stilts. The ghoul in the lead thumped rapidly until he positioned himself in the front of the Assay office. He had a metal plate hanging over his chest by a chain. It was Roy. He had changed his old hat for a large sombrero, probably because it protected his head better from tossed silver dust. The metal plate was for silver bullets. Roy was perched on his stilts like a parrot between limbs. The stilts would be for walking on a silver-dust floor.

"All right," Roy called. "Might as well come on out and get eaten. We'll make it quick. Mostly. Quill wants it done now, so go on and butter and salt up your asses, and get on out here. Be best for us if you take your clothes off first. Easier to eat."

"We ain't got any butter," Wild Bill said, and laughed loudly.

"Well, just come on out. We'll go it dry. That's the usual."

"Yeah, it's alright dry," said a voice from the crowd.

Smith counted. There were at least a dozen men on stilts, ready to go, and several men and women and children were carrying a pair, prepared to mount up when the time came.

"They appear to be less stupid than they look," Payday said.

"Back to the stairs," Smith said. "We have silver in the office up there, and it's a narrow path. It's our best choice... Ah hell."

A shadow large enough to shade a wide portion of the ghouls passed along the street. Though they didn't see the source, the shadow was obviously made by Quill.

"Why doesn't he go straight to the tower?" Wild Bill said.

"I figure he's got certain restrictions until the time is right," Smith said. "He's powerful, but he doesn't set the rules. That would be The Old Ones. Rules that make sense to them and don't make any sense to us. Quill's waiting us out until The Old Ones are in position to enter into our realm. If we can't get to the tower, Quill certainly can, and whenever he's ready. So he doesn't need to be there right now. He's like the gatekeeper, and my guess is he's waiting on the key, of sorts, to make the final event happen."

"I don't get it," The Kid said. "The Old Ones are more powerful than he is. How does he think they're going to let him rule things, or even have a place at the table?"

"The part of him that's the old Quill sees an angle, I guess," Smith said. "Gamblers are like that. And he was a gambler as well as a shithead. Thing is, he wasn't that good a gambler, but he was one marvelous shithead. Ought to know. Takes one to know one."

"Seems to hold all the cards now," Wild Bill said. "Course, he could be holding aces and eights. They didn't work out for me, so let's hope that's his hand."

"If he gets to play that hand, it might turn out all right for him," Smith said. "We got to see he doesn't get the chance to put his cards on the table."

With a wild whoop the ghouls came stiff-walking forward on their stilts, and the others that were holding theirs, with the assistance of unstilted ghouls, climbed into position.

"To the stairs," Smith said. "On the stairway we can narrow their progress, hold them off better."

The defenders raced to the stairs.

It was a short wait. They could see Roy's boots on the stilt supports in the doorway, and then Roy stopped.

"Damn it," he said. "Rabbit shit."

It was obvious what the situation was. He had made the stilts too tall to get through the door. He clumped off down the boardwalk cursing.

"Okay," Payday said. "Maybe they are just as dumb as they look."

But others were climbing in through the window, carrying their stilts, mounting them as they stepped through, being pushed upright by ghouls from the outside. The first to actually stand mounted in the Assay office was an old woman wearing a bonnet and men's pants and boots. Tobacco stains covered her teeth and ran down the side of her face and over the front of her dress. She started briskly toward them on the stilts. Payday stepped down a step on the stairs, close to the bottom, and when the old woman was close, she tossed a handful of silver dust at her. The dust hit its mark. The old woman let out a kind of squeak, started dissolving. Her head collapsed and so did the rest of her. It ran down through her clothes and over the stilts and to the floor. The stilts, no longer supported, wobbled and collapsed to the floor with a clatter.

In through the door and in through the windows came more ghouls on stilts, shorter stilts than Roy had. The back door groaned and cracked, swung open, and pretty soon the ghouls were coming in from there as well, clumping about as if they were a herd of elephants.

Payday raced back upstairs, came out of the office dragging along four more heavy bags of silver. Cameahwait cut the tie strings open with his knife.

The ghouls clomped toward the stairs. Smith and the others tossed silver dust. Ghouls dissolved. Yet, they kept coming, endless waves on stilts, and outside could be heard the sound of hammering and sawing and new stilts being made. It was such a frantic sound, had the situation been less perilous, it might have been amusing.

And then in through the door came Roy. He had on his wide sombrero and his steel chest plate, but now he had found curled, wooden, roofing shingles, and had fastened them about his legs with leather straps. He had shortened his stilts by sawing them off at the bottom. It was an uneven sawing, and he wobbled a bit. He came stomping his stilts through the midst of the others, yelled out, "Now you're done. Now it's all over but the chewing."

Smith pulled a handful of dust and tossed it at Roy. It hit the breast plate and scattered, bits of it burning holes in Roy's shirt sleeve and arm, but he was not seriously damaged.

That's when Cameahwait cut down on him with one of the shotgun barrels. The force of it knocked Roy back and clipped off one stilt at boot level. Roy slammed into the floor and silver dust floated up in a cloud and came down on him in a mist. It hit Roy's face, arms, slipped beneath his breast plate and singed his rotting flesh.

"Shit," Roy said. "If that don't beat all."

Within instants, there was nothing left of Roy but silver dust, a metal plate, shingles, a sombrero, and some empty boots.

"You dumb dead bastard," The Kid said.

For a moment everything had been frozen, as if in ice, but now there were bullets flying from the ghouls on stilts. Others shot at the defenders from the windows, sometimes shooting into their own group, most of the bullets passing through them like mosquitoes through air. Wild Bill took a burning shot through his left side, one that went through like an ice pick jab and slammed into the stairs.

Silver bullets were fired by the defenders and the ghouls fell, but still others came, and now the Assay office was full of their stilts, yells, and bullets. They wobbled, tangled together, and fell by the handfuls. But plenty still stood, and new ones were coming through the doors and windows, and they were starting up the stairs, backing up the defenders. With bullets flying and the silver dust in the bags growing low, Smith grabbed Shadow's reins, led him up the stairs. The others backed up and into the office, firing as they went, slammed the door and threw the lock. They shoved the desk against the door. Shadow, who had been waiting in the office as quiet as a clerk, made a snorting sound.

"That won't hold long," Wild Bill said, pulling his shirt out from his wound.

"Bill, you okay?" Smith asked.

"Right as rain," Wild Bill said. "I've had worse holes than this. Well, now, wait a minute. Not true. This one is a doozy."

"Anyone else hit?" Smith said.

Amazingly, no one was, not even Shadow, who Smith felt, big as he was, would have been a prime target.

"Not only are they dead and stupid," Payday said. "But they can't shoot either."

"Horse shit on floor," Cameahwait said.

Sure enough, he had.

There was a loud squalling sound outside the window, and then there was a shadow that filled the open double window like an avalanche of coal. Quill lit on the sill like some sort of mythological gryphon, folding his wings tight around him, bending his body to allow his odd-shaped head to peek inside, to see the defenders. Behind him the moon was growing darker and the warm air was blowing around Quill's body and in through the window. With the wind came a stench like a pit packed full of rotting corpses and all the sewage of the world. To make matters worse, the room already smelled like horseshit.

Quill showed a bizarre smile of many sharp teeth, and there was about his eyes and face a look of confidence, as if he were already swapping spit with The Old Ones.

(7)

Shadow rose up on his back legs and kicked his silver horseshoes at Quill, but Smith snatched his reins and pulled him back.

Quill didn't flinch. Quill licked his chops with a long, black tongue, and eyed them through narrow, yellow slits. Not only was he smiling, but there were so many teeth some of them were poking crookedly through the sides of his jaws.

The defenders gathered together in a near huddle, like cattle grouping together, and stared at Quill, weapons pointed, waiting for Quill to explode into a fury of leather wings and slashing claws. But he didn't move. He merely remained perched.

Intimidation, thought Smith? Maybe Quill was doing what he was doing just because he could. He wanted to make their skin crawl and was savoring his win, the admittance of The Old Ones into this segment of the world, and finally into the wider world beyond, waiting here for the moon to shift, darken and die.

"Fools," Quill said, and his voice seemed to come from somewhere deep and muddy. "The strong always win."

"Who says we aren't strong?" Smith said.

Quill chuckled in a manner that sounded like gravel being ground beneath a wheel, but Smith thought he detected something else in that sound as well that didn't fit the confident look on his face. Uncertainty? Fear?

"You seem nervous Quill," Smith said. "Why don't you come on inside? I mean, you're too powerful for our silver dust, right?"

"Your silly charms have no effect on me," Quill said.

That's when Cameahwait grabbed the scoop containing silver dust and flung it onto Quill. The silver spread wide as if it were a tiny storm, hit Quill with a splashing sound. Little black dots smoked on his leather skin. Quill let out a squawk and his wings flapped rapidly, then he shook momentarily. He didn't dissolve, nor did he move from his perch, but it was obvious the attack was painful. Curls of smoke drifted up from the burns on Quill's body.

Cameahwait's leathery face cracked in a smile.

Shadow made a sound that almost sounded like laughter.

"So you got a little more bark on you than them dead folks got," Wild Bill said. "But you look hurt to me. I think you figure you'll run the clock out without putting your ass on the line. That's what I figure. I think you think we might just kill your ass."

"That's a nice little speech," Quill said. "But I merely mean to enjoy your last moments. For all of you, it's all over but the rendering."

"Rendering doesn't sound good," The Kid said.

Quill gathered himself, folded his wings again, and bent his body to stick his head through the window more deeply. "I want to see my little minions tear you apart. That's the rendering, and then if there's anything left, The Old Ones will enjoy that, and what they enjoy lasts forever."

Then came a banging at the door, and the door heaved against the desk, but the lock held. Shadow stirred, whirled about in frustration.

"There's someone knocking now," Quill said.

Smith thought again: Why hasn't Quill come inside?

Smith glanced down and saw that there were little piles and spreads of silver on the floor, under the window, throughout the room. Silver that had fallen from the bags they had taken to use against the ghouls, maybe some left over from when the Assay Office was in a panic. There were those big chunks, and the silver trim. Silver might not be the end all for Quill as it was for the ghouls, but it had hurt him, and now it was causing him to maintain his spot on the sill, in spite of what he was saying.

"It will all soon come to an end," Quill said, and when he spoke shadows came out of his mouth and moved into the room and danced along the walls and faded.

"You really think this is going to work like they're the bank owners and you're bank president?" Smith said. "And maybe later you come to own the bank yourself? I get the idea that The Old Ones aren't exactly grateful types."

Quill didn't answer, just sat there on the still. The ghouls shoving and banging at the door intensified. The desk moved a little, scraping the floor.

Smith moved to the desk, opened the drawer quickly, pulled out a large nugget of silver. He turned toward Quill, whose attention was on that nugget.

"This worries you some, doesn't it?" Smith said.

"That can't kill me," Quill said. "You should know that by now."

"Yeah," Smith said, "but I think that's because it's in small amounts, but maybe big amounts worry you a little more. This room is full of silver dust, ore, trim, and I bet you a lot of these ornaments are silver too. As a gambling man, I'm going to bet that much concentrated silver is something you fear. The dust, that's like ant bites. But this chunk, I got a feeling it can do more."

Wild Bill had his hand pressed to his side. A lot of blood was leaking around his fingers. "Since I'm starting to feel mite weak, it's time to fish or cut bait."

Wild Bill snatched the nugget from Smith's hand, and charged Quill with it.

Bill hit Quill like a train might hit a cow on the tracks. He hit him solid, and he stuck the silver ore at him, tagged him with it right between the eyes. A burst of flame flared from Quill's head, and Wild Bill's momentum carried Quill back and out of the window. Bill fell after, clutching at Quill with one hand, hanging on tight. With his free arm and an overhand looping motion, he slammed the ore into Quill's open mouth, past those rows of teeth and deep into Quill's throat.

A blast of flame came out of Quill's mouth and burst from his ass in a fart of fire, and then Quill soared up. Smith and Payday and The Kid crowded the window to look up.

"Goddamn, Bill," Smith said.

Behind him, Cameahwait said, "Done good."

Up went Quill, Wild Bill dangling by one hand, precariously clutching one of Quill's large neck scales. Now Bill brought up both hands and grabbed, was able to loop both arms around Quill's neck completely. Bill dangled under the high flying monster's neck like a pendant on a necklace.

Higher Quill rose. Higher. Still coughing and farting fire from that nugget.

"So he's not so immune to silver," Payday said. "We just needed a large patch of it."

Quill shivered violently in the air, beat his wings and twisted his body. Wild Bill came loose. It was a long fall. They heard Bill hit the top of a building with a loud thump and a red mist of blood puffed up and filled the air above the building and settled.

Quill, still shooting fire from both ends, was now high up and flying away from them, heading toward the tower.

"Quill's had enough of us," The Kid said.

"It's time," Smith said. "Look."

The moon had turned from dark to blood red.

"Wild Bill didn't sacrifice himself like that for us to stand here jawing," Payday said.

"That's right," The Kid said. "You and Payday, go for the tower. Me and Cameahwait will take up the rear, keep you covered best we can. Cause distraction for as long as we can."

The lock on the door snapped. The desk moved forward slightly. Through the crack in the door they could see the faces of the dead. The faces were high up, as the ghouls were still on stilts. There were flashes of teeth, a bit of dying moonlight falling onto their eyes. Then they stopped, sniffed at the room like dogs sniffing at the hunt. They squealed and moved back.

"They won't come through there," Smith said. "If Quill didn't like it, they won't be able to stand it at all."

Smith looked out at the roof tops of the buildings that ran from the Assay Office toward the hill and the bell tower. Smith said, "I got a plan. You don't like it, I'm all ears for another. But this one, it's all I got."

"So far your plans have been a little less than complicated," Payday said. "And I don't mean that in a good way."

"I'm kind of a straightforward fellow," Smith said.

"Talk fast," said Cameahwait.

Smith reached into the open safe and grabbed the remaining bags of silver.

"To start with," he said. "I'm going to need these, ~~as well~~ AND as many large chunks of silver as I can reasonably stuff in my saddlebags."

⟨8⟩

On the landing the ghouls became brave again, pushed at the door, trying to slide the desk back, and then suddenly there was nothing to push against and the door flew open and the ghouls in the front toppled on their stilts and came crashing to the floor, covered in a film of silver. A puff of white smoke rose up from the floor as those ghouls dissolved and others clumped in, and then Cameahwait let loose with the shotgun and temporarily cleared a path. For a moment it was as if a tornado had blown through the ghouls.

But all that silver. It was too much. The ghouls stomped backwards on their stilts, not up to dealing with it, same as their boss.

Smith mounted Shadow, charged the door, leaning close to Shadow's neck so that he could make the passage. Shadow blew out of the room like a black storm, hit the landing going too fast, smashed through the railing and plunged to the floor below. Any other horse would have broken a leg, but the great beast took the fall in stride, slid on the silver dust on the floor, wheeled, dashed for the front door, cut through the stilt-walking ghouls, causing them and their wooden props to fly about as if part of a circus trick.

Shadow rushed through the front door and through the smoke from the dissolving ghouls. Bullets were fired by the ghouls that were still on stilts and able, other shots were fired by ghouls standing on the boardwalk and in the street, but except for one shot that grazed Shadow's ear and clipped the bottom of Smith's gun holster, they made it fine, blew out into the street in a swirl of dust, wheeled, and galloped away without damage.

Smith stuck the reins in his teeth, and pulled his pistols.

Payday had already started across the roofs, the way Smith planned. She made the first leap from the window of the Assay Office to the lower lying building next door without much effort, but the next leap was wider, and she almost missed, was barely able to scramble onto the roof, her boot heels scratching at the tiles and sliding her back. She clawed her way up, struggled to her feet, and ran across the roofing. She had bound her guns down with the hammer loops, and as she ran she reached down to check. Both were still in the holsters.

So far, so good.

Glancing down into the street, Payday saw Shadow darting by with ghouls grasping at him and Smith. They were being tossed aside by the cannon-like shot of the galloping horse, or being dragged and flung away as they tried to grab hold of Smith or the saddle. It was an amazing view, that great horse and Smith with the reins in his teeth, firing his revolvers, the ghouls falling away like wheat beneath the scythe.

Payday paused, pulled her pistols, began firing down on the dead, dropping ghouls. Every shot counted. She had never shot so well. She felt brave enough to run along the roof top and shoot. So involved was she in the shooting, she almost didn't manage enough spring in her legs to leap to the next rooftop. But she did make it, barely, and then she was staggering on the roof, wooden shingles coming loose beneath her boots, causing her to skid, but she regained her footing, saw out in the street that Smith had burst through and was well ahead of the ghouls who were rushing behind him. She looked at the tower. Visible to the sides of the tower, the moon was no longer red like fresh, hot blood; it had turned coppery, like a drying wound.

The Kid and Cameahwait gave Payday the allotted head start, and then they went out the window, leaping to the lower roof, then running along it, and leaping to the next, and then the next. They were the third wave. Smith and Shadow first, then Payday, and then the two of them. The idea was to split the focus of the ghouls until Smith could reach the tower.

As they ran along a roof top, in the distance they could see Payday, running and leaping from roof to roof, and then she jumped from one high roof to a lower one, and was out of sight.

The living dead, in all manner of conditions, reasonably fresh, partially rotten, some with legs and arms, some missing one or the other, some ghouls little more than a head with thin, blackened, parchment-like skin over their bones, went yipping and yelling, growling, running, walking, and in some cases crawling, as fast as each could go toward the bell tower and the darkening moon.

The air had begun to tremble.

PART SIX:

The Tower

The ringing of a bell and odd words spoken aloud,
will never serve to surpass the wonder of a woman's sigh.
JERSEY FITZGERALD

⟨1⟩

As Cameahwait and The Kid ran along the roofs, they were spotted from below. A ghoul firing a Winchester missed them, but hit one of the wooden shingles just as The Kid's boots stepped on it, and away he slid, over the side of the roof and down into the street, a hard, painful drop that knocked the wind out of him. For a moment he lay there stunned, unable to crawl, his pistols thrown from his hands.

Cameahwait leaped from the roof, shotgun in his hands. It was a drop he was ready for, and he took it well, came up from a crouch, still holding the gun. The ghouls were gathering around them. The Kid was up now, finding his pistols, as the crowd of ghouls grew thicker, distracted from the tower by the opportunity of a free meal of Shoshone and white boy.

The Kid and Cameahwait pushed their backs to the building wall.

Cameahwait laughed and began to sing his death song in the language of the Shoshone.

The Kid glanced at him. Cameahwait's voice was loud and clear.

"What the hell?" The Kid said, and began to sing as loud as he could, "On Top Of Old Smokey."

And now the ghouls came and the songs ended. Cameahwait cut down with one barrel of the shotgun, cutting a swathe through them with the silver loads, and then he cut down again with the second barrel with similar results.

The Kid fired both revolvers, hitting what he aimed at, re-killing the dead. But it was hopeless. He and the Cameahwait had only pushed them back for a moment, created a gap for a few instants. They ghouls were already regrouping, and there were too many.

Cameahwait reloaded, opened up with one barrel, and then the other, cutting an even wider gap through the monsters. Again, it was momentary.

The Kid looked at Cameahwait.

Cameahwait looked at him.

"I ain't going be one of them," The Kid said, and he grinned a little. The grin quivered only slightly.

Cameahwait made a sound that might have been a grunt. His expression didn't change. He reached out a hand, and The Kid, who had managed to put one fresh bullet in both revolvers, gave Cameahwait one of them.

As the ghouls swarmed them they pressed their pistols against each other's foreheads and pulled the triggers in unison.

Payday was on the roof of a low shed near the church. She saw Smith riding along, soon to be near the wall of the shed. She called out to him. He looked up, yelled, "Jump."

It wasn't a long drop, ten feet, but it was a bit precarious to try and jump from there onto the back of the horse. But, then again, she had done similar stunts many times in the circus. She saw the ghouls coming along the street. One of them was wearing The Kid's hat.

"Damn it," she said.

She made sure her guns were tight in their holsters, pulled her coil of whip tighter over her shoulder, and jumped.

And missed.

She landed on her ass just behind Shadow, knocking the breath out of her.

"Quit screwing around," Smith yelled at her, wheeling the horse back to her.

Gathering herself, Payday leaped to her feet and sprang to the back of the horse. Smith put his heels to Shadow's ribs, and away they went, both of them hanging onto the critter for dear life. When Shadow reached the tower, he bounded up the stone steps, and then pausing before the closed doors, reared up and slammed his front hooves into the wood, swinging the doors wide open. Down came Shadow with a clatter of hooves, and raced them into the cool dark of the church.

Dismounting, Smith and Payday shoved the church doors closed. The door had not been barred, but now they picked up the long, wooden rail against the wall, and fitted it in the hooks on either side, and no sooner had they done so, than the door rocked with the pounding of fists, the kicking of feet, accompanied by the howling and screaming and calling of the dead. The doors strained against the wooden barrier.

Smith and Payday turned and saw the stairway that led up to the bell tower. It was narrow and rickety looking. Smith whistled Shadow over, and they climbed astride the horse again. Up the stairs they went, Shadow climbing the squeaking steps swiftly and sure-footed as a mountain goat.

Outside and above the tower, Quill dropped down from the darkening sky, and landed on the tip of the tower. Above him a few stars wavered. Others winked out. The moon, so full, was darker than ever now. The copper color was turning black as sin.

Quill fluttered his wings and lifted his head. There was a spot in the sky that was starting to rip, ever so slightly, and there was movement in the rip, and very briefly what looked like a tentacle slipped from the crack, waved in the sky, then slipped back inside. The crack closed, opened again, closed. But each time it opened, the rip was wider.

Quill folded his wings about him and waited for the moment when he would make his move and cause the rip to tear the sky wide, and the Old Ones would enter.

As Smith and Payday made the top of the stairs and Shadow came to stand on the platform near the great bell that hung there, the air turned sour, and down below the ghouls pounded even harder. Smith and Payday could hear the doorway creak and crack and start to sag. Dead fingers wiggled through the split between the doors as the thick, wooden bar began to give.

Payday looked down and sighed.

"One pile of shit, and then another," she said.

"Yep," Smith said.

Outside they heard a sound like the heaving and plummeting of something mountain-sized. Through the gaps on the tower they could see out, and the air rippled and darkened, then shimmered gradually back to normal.

"The time has come," Payday said.

"Not if we can do what we came here to do," Smith said, moving about the bell, looking this way and that.

"Exactly what is that?"

"The spell. We have to destroy the spell."

"How?"

"Snappy was a little short on specifics," Smith said. "Something to do with proper protocol, I believe, for whatever sense that might make. Hey. Wait a minute."

"We don't really have any waiting time," Payday said. "You got something, it's time to bring that buddy out, or we're going to be serving The Old Ones dinner with a side of horse."

"The bell," he said.

It was beginning to glow red, as if heated in a forge. Smith bent down and looked inside the bell. There were rows and rows of crude markings, but the mere sight of them made Smith ill; they were evil personified. This was the place of power, the weakest point in the cosmos, a place through which The Old Ones could enter. All it took was the spell, and Quill had placed the spell in the bell, waiting for the right time when it would open the gate for The Old Ones.

Below, the doors to the church burst open as the restraining plank snapped in half.

"The silver," Smith said. "It's in the saddle bags. Put some of it on the stairs, mid-way and up."

As Smith moved around the bell, trying to figure what to do, Payday pulled one of the silver bags out of a saddle bag, tore it open, bolted down the stairs until she was halfway, and began to sprinkle the steps with silver, retreated up to the landing, spreading it on the stairs as she went.

Outside, at the peak of the tower, Quill had began to chant the spell. That, thought Payday was the final touch. The spell in the bell, and then the spell out of Quill's mouth.

When she came back up the stairs and reached the landing, Quill's chanting had reached an ear-splitting level and the air was growing thick. It was hard to breath, hard to swallow.

The ghouls were starting up the stairs, reaching the dust, their feet seeming to suck the silver up through their boots and shoes, dissolving them, causing them to tumble into their comrades and drip them to the floor below in an oily mess.

Payday said, "Dust or no dust, they keep coming, they'll make it up here in time."

"We got to bring out the big boys," Smith said.

Near the tip of the tower the sky had lowered and darkened and lost all the stars. The rip was broadening and there were glimpses of indescribable things that moved inside of it. Quill could literally reach up and touch the sky now, and the night was like touching aging sail canvas. As Quill chanted, his talons tore at that fabric, desperately trying to rip it wide open while he chanted, the spell giving him the ability to do just that.

"...saggoth, ciptoid, cthulhu..."

Smith pulled a stick of dynamite and a fuse from his saddle bags, cut it in two with his knife, poked the fuse into it, produced a match, struck it on the side of his pants with one determined pull. He studied the flame for an instant, lit the fuse, held it in front of him, staring at it.

"Shouldn't you throw it?" Payday said.

"Not yet."

"How about now?"

"Not yet."

When the fuse was little more than a suggestion, Smith dropped it over the side, down onto the stairway and the clamoring ghouls that were trying to come fast enough to bypass the silver which ate up through their boots into their feet and melted them down.

The explosion blasted the stairs and the ghouls into wet fragments. The platform on which they stood rocked and rang the giant bell violently. The clapper slammed back and forth inside the bell and the noise was deafening. Smith and Payday and Shadow were knocked about the landing, but managed not to fall.

Still, the platform was sagging to one side. Shadow scrambled to maintain his footing, and so did Smith and Payday.

With a sag and a creak, the platform inched back into proper position, but was less stable.

On the tower the blast shook Quill from where he was crouched, sent him hurtling through the thickening air. Quill squalled and dove for one of the openings in the bell tower, looked inside at Smith and Payday, the pawing Shadow.

For a hot moment it looked as if Quill was going to charge into the tower and finish them, but instead he stuck his head forward and let out a scream that would have made lesser humans die of fright. The bell even moved. Shadow kicked up his front legs and came down on the other side of the bell with heavy force. The bell swung out and hit Quill solidly, knocked him flapping out into the darkness, out of view.

"Quill spared us," Payday said. "He didn't come inside."

"Shadow helped with that," Smith said. "But mainly he's got bigger fish to fry."

Above them Smith and Payday heard the chant begin again. That was why Smith thought Quill hadn't bothered to rip them from limb to limb. Same as them, he was on a time schedule, and it was growing short. His window for letting The Old Ones in could close if the spell were not completed during the right measure of time; those crawling words from an ancient book that had been hidden and embedded inside the bell had their moment, and their moment was now. It was now or never for Quill and The Old Ones.

At least that's how Smith figured it. It was a guess, but it was all he had.

(2)

Smith stood on the edge of the platform and looked down. There was meat and wood and things unidentifiable the dynamite had blown all over the church. It looked like a tornado had been through it.

The chanting had reached a tremendous volume above them, and now there was an echo from it, as if the universe had grown hollow. Smith turned to Payday. "I need your bullets."

"Bullets?"

"And now."

Payday quickly unfastened her gun belt and gave it to Smith.

"This isn't going to turn out well for us anyway we go, is it?" she said.

"No," Smith said. "But the world might get a fair shake."

"Good enough," Payday said.

Smith flung the belt over his shoulder, and then removed the saddle bags from Shadow. He opened them up. Inside, several sticks of dynamite remained, as well as silver dust and small chunks of silver ore. He began pinching the bullets from Payday's gun belt and dropping them into the saddle bag with the dynamite. Smith then emptied his gun belt into the bag. The silver bullets, the silver dust and ore, along with the dynamite, filled the bag to bulging.

"You might climb down one the support posts," Smith said, "get as far away from here as possible."

"Doubt I'd get too far before the dead caught up with me, and if you do blow Quill to hell, and that stops them, well… You won't be with me."

"That's a fact."

"I might get a splinter in my thighs shimming down one of those support posts."

"A possibility."

"I'll stay."

Smith nodded. "All right then. Listen to me. Quill, he doesn't want anything to happen to this bell because the spell is inside it, and when he chants it, it activates it even more, which I think is the plan. He's got to heat it up by chanting, so to speak. I want to make sure it goes and he goes with it. So you take the bell rope, and when I tell you, start ringing it. Not before I say, though."

"I can do that," Payday said.

"It'll take some work."

"I'm up for it."

Smith removed one stick of dynamite from the saddle bags without taking them off his shoulder. He put the stick between his teeth and sought out a match. When he found one, he took the stick of dynamite out of his mouth and said, "Ring that son-of-a-bitch."

The rope to the bell was coiled on the landing, near the gap where the bell hung. Payday took hold of it, and before she could pull the rope and ring the bell, Smith climbed up in one of the openings to the bell tower.

The bell gave out with a thunderous ring.

In the tower the sound was almost deafening.

Quill's chanting couldn't be heard above the sound of the bell. The bell was much louder. Quill flapped his wings and moved away from the peak of the tower until he could ~~took~~ hover and look in one of the bell tower gaps, and standing there in the gap was Smith, grinning around a stick of dynamite between his teeth.

Smith held up a match, and just as he struck it along the side of his pants, Quill dove for him. It was an incredibly fast dive. Quill's wings beat rapidly, and then Quill was on Smith, banging him back against the side of the bell, which knocked him rolling to the very edge of the platform. The dynamite dropped from Smith's mouth and rolled along the platform. Smith's hat fell through the gap below the bell. The saddlebags slipped off his shoulder and skidded beside him.

Shadow, excited by all the commotion, rose up on his hind legs and struck at the bell, swinging it out of line, causing the platform to shudder. Smith managed to his knees, grabbed the saddle bags, slung them over his shoulder again, and hustled along on his hands and knees after the loose stick of dynamite which was at the very edge of the platform. Smith grabbed it just as Quill, hovering above him, yanked him up with his sharp talons and flung him back against the bell, causing Smith to lose the stick of dynamite again. It rolled along the platform toward Payday, who put her foot on it, but it slipped from beneath her boot and fell down the gap below the bell.

Quill tried to maneuver around the bell, even as Payday continued to tug at the rope and swing the bell, making it a difficult affair for him. Quill gave that up and bent down and grabbed one of Smith's legs. Quill smiled those many teeth. His tongue slipped out of his mouth and slapped at the air. His eyes narrowed.

He lifted Smith up by his leg, held him above him and looked up at him, opened his mouth as if to lower Smith's head into it.

There was a cracking sound, and Payday's whip wrapped around Quill's neck. Continuing to hold Smith aloft, Quill used his free hand to peel the whip off his neck and snatch it from Payday's hand. Payday grabbed at the bell rope, swung the loose end and sent the heavy rope smashing against the side of Quill's head, causing it to wrap around his neck, just as the bell swung away from him. Surprised, Quill was pulled toward the gap in the tower, and through it he went, losing his grip on Smith in the process. Smith almost went through the gap, but not quite. He fell and lay close to the edge and looked up into the bell. The words that had been hidden inside were blood-red and sun-yellow and there were hopping strands of green fire. Smith couldn't tell if that meant the spell was still in progress or coming apart.

He couldn't chance it.

Smith still had the saddle bags. He quickly removed another stick of dynamite from one the bags, stuck it between his teeth.

Quill rose up on beating wings beneath the bell, hit the rim of it so hard the entire tower rocked. With spread wings, he couldn't manage his way back through the gap now that the bell was no longer swinging, but instead hung solid over the space beneath it.

The sky seemed less dark. The air less foul and cold. Something was changing, but Smith couldn't tell if it was for the better or the worse. There was still a loud tearing sound above the tower. Glancing through a gap in the tower, Smith saw a long green tentacle wriggle in the air, slap against the tower, then flash away. For a moment there was a great bulging eye shining out of the rip, and then it too was gone.

Payday joined Smith, leading Shadow. Smith climbed into the Shadow's saddle, and pulled Payday up behind him. He produced another match from his shirt pocket, prepared to strike it. Payday reached around and took the match from him. She popped it alight with her thumb nail.

Quill's talons appeared at the edge of the opening beneath the bell. His head showed next. He pushed the bell back with one great clawed hand, making a gap for him to slip through, his wings folded tight against his back.

Smith turned slightly in the saddle so that he was looking back at Payday. She lit the dynamite in his mouth. Smith turned and faced forward. Payday wrapped her arms around him and pushed up tight against him.

The fuse fizzled.

Quill came through the opening and rose up in the air with a beat of wings, and just as he was about to dive down on Smith and Payday and Shadow, the dynamite blew.

When the stick in Smith's mouth exploded, it caused the rest of the dynamite to blow, scattering silver dust, ore and bullets. For one hot, fiery moment the air was full of flying silver, meat and dynamite blast. The bell cracked and rang and flew out of one of the gaps in the tower, came apart in midair, tossing the colorful shapes of the spell inside the bell in all directions, fading the colors to black and then crumbling, gray ash.

The tower rocked, creaked and groaned, came loose of the church, and down it went, tearing free in great slabs of adobe, mortar and stone, striking the street, throwing up great clouds of swirling dust. The ghouls that weren't smashed flat by the falling tower, the ones standing in the street, extending from the edge of the tower's ruins all the way back to the Assay office, shook, and came apart, and up from them came a great and collective sigh that was caught up on a swiftly passing wind, and the ruins of the ghouls were carried away by it.

Above it all, the sky, which had been so close, rose up. The rip sealed itself with a lip-smacking sound. Stars popped into place, and the moon, like a blister popping, swelled and exploded into—

Daylight.

The sun shone apple-red on the horizon. Birds chirped. The wind lifted and it was fresh and warm, and it whispered through the forests, whispered on through Fallen Rock, along the deserted streets and alleys.

Behind where the bell tower had stood, on the ground, there was a fragment of the bell. There were still little shapes inside of it; the shapes were gray and they shimmered and crawled.

A curious rabbit hopped out of the grass onto the fragment, nosed it, touched the curious shapes, and—

SPUT

The rabbit was gone. Rabbit hair swirled about for a moment and drifted to the ground. The shapes inside the bell ceased to move, turned stiff, and slid off the bell and into the grass, now dry and dead and powerless.

POSTSCRIPT
AND RESURRECTION

And Lazarus rose. But he didn't smell all that good.
SO SAYS SNAPPY

(1)

The door to Hell's Saloon flew open and a wheelbarrow containing what was left of Smith was rolled in by the near-naked blonde. She dumped him in the middle of the floor. The pieces of meat steamed and twisted and linked together like a puzzle, and an instant later Smith stood up where the pile had been, fully dressed, his gun belt on, his hat in his hand.

As the blonde disappeared back through the door pushing the wheelbarrow, Smith saw Snappy behind the bar. Already he was pouring Smith a drink.

"Toss one back?" Snappy said.

"Don't mind if I do," Smith said.

As he did, he looked in the mirror and saw that he looked even younger and stronger than he had looked before Snappy had transformed him. Behind his reflection, shadows moved in the mirror.

He heard a loud noise that could only be one thing. A fart. He turned, and there was Belle Star sitting in a chair at the poker table with Quantrail, Blood Billy, Jesse James and Hickok. Belle had one hip lifted. She said, "Damn, that was sticky."

Smith was sure that none of them had been there the moment before. In fact, neither had the table and chairs been present.

Wild Bill tipped his hat. Smith tipped his back.

The others smiled. Except Bloody Bill. He studied his cards.

"Where are the others?" Smith said.

"They went somewhere else," Snappy said. "Cameahwait had the Happy Hunting grounds as his reward. It's a kind of a subdivision, and The Kid, well, he got the pearly gates, though that's just what they're called. No pearls are involved."

"Doc? Undertaker? Double Shot?" He wanted to ask about Payday, but didn't. He feared the answer might not be what he hoped for.

"They went where The Kid went."

"Good. That means we won. Right? We did win?"

Snappy reached under the bar and brought out a small, scorched gold box with all manner of writing embedded into it. The box was wrapped in thick twine with a bow knot tied in the center.

"Zelzarda?" Smith said. "Alias, Quill?"

"Yep, that's him," Snappy said.

"Well, I suggest a better knot, that boy's trouble."

"Oh, he's been taken care of. Of that you can assure yourself."

Smith nodded. "By the way. I did what you asked. Don't I get a better shake than a drink in Hell?"

The door through which Smith had seen Bull and the Frenchman go some long time back, blew open and flames curled out. Bodies on hooks held by invisible powers swirled about on display, amidst groans and screams of such pain and horror, Smith felt the hairs on his head lift his hat.

"It could be worse for you," Snappy said.

"It could indeed," Smith said.

The door Smith had come through flew open again, and the blonde came in pushing the wheelbarrow. It was heaped with smoking flesh and leather fragments, a whip and an eye patch lay on top of the pile. Smith's heart began to beat fast.

The big blonde dumped it sizzling onto the floor and retreated back through the door.

Within an instant Payday rose up from it, fully formed, the whip coiled over her shoulder, wearing her eye patch, her guns strapped on.

Smith grinned.

She too looked younger, fresher. Her hair was tied back in a ponytail and she looked good in her tight leather clothes and boots.

"Wait a minute," Smith said, whirling to face Snappy. "She doesn't deserve to be here."

Snappy grinned, and something unidentifiable, but definitely alive and moving, crawled behind his eyes. "I couldn't agree more."

The door banged open again, and through it came the blonde, pushing the wheelbarrow. It was full of smoking horse hair and hooves with silver shoes nailed to them. She tipped the wheelbarrow, and—

(2)

The night was a crawling black velvet of sounds. The stars were bright like candles, and the moon was full and high, and there was not a cloud in the sky. The light from moon and stars shown down on the mouth of an old abandoned, boarded-over mine shaft.

Down deep in the mine came the sound of echoing horse hooves, growing louder as they neared. A thick finger of light rose out of the shaft and flickered through the cracks in the boards, and down in the mine, within the light, were the slatted-shadows of a man and a woman riding a large horse. The shadows roared out of the mouth of the cave, bursting the boards wide and far, gathered and formed and were now a topless roadster, black as the deepest pits of the earth, except for flame licks on the side and theatrical silver markings on the front that formed the word SHADOW. The light came from the headlights of the car. Out jumped the roadster, far out of the mine, jumped to radio music played in three-quarter time. Smith was at the wheel, hatless, dark hair greased back into a big ducks-ass, and beside him sat Payday in a dress the color of the one Smith had given her, but now it was a green poodle dress. Her hair was tied back in a pony tail and the wind whipped it like a flag. She no longer had on the patch. She didn't need it. She looked more beautiful that the first day Smith saw her in the bar, before Quill did what he did.

At the base of the mine was a dirt road. Smith braked the machine to a tire-burning stop. The engine made a noise like the whinny of a horse. Smith turned in the seat and smiled at Payday.

"By the way," Payday said. "What's your real name?"

"Smith."

She laughed.

Smith gunned the roadster, spun it in a show-off circle, then geared it and gassed it, and rode it hard. They rounded a curve, and there, high and bright in the roadsters headlights, was a billboard that read: FALLING ROCK FIRST NATIONAL BANK. AUTO LOANS. On the sign was the painting of an Edsel Sedan, a shiny, 1950's car with a chrome, rear-end panel.

Down the hill they went, seemingly about to drive right into the sign. Payday looked up and saw it, said, "Well, I'll be damned."

"Not today," Smith said, as he steered around a curve, passed the billboard, blasted down the road in the roaring roadster, the radio playing a hot little number, eight beats to the bar.

The tail lights of the roadster showed red and bright, then less bright, and then they were gone and the music lingered, then it too died out, and there was only the high night sky and the bright moonlight, and all of those shiny and perfect stars.